"Do you wonder what it would be like between us now?"

He sure as hell did, ever since she'd walked out of Colt's barn. That image had kept Reed awake more than one night since he'd returned.

"No." Her expressive eyes and her breathy voice contradicted her statement.

"I do." His lips pressed against the tender skin behind her ear, and he felt her shiver. How long had it been since he'd felt a real connection with a woman?

Not since he'd left Avery.

Her head rested on his shoulder, and her warmth seeped into him. Need overrode what little common sense he possessed. His lips traced a path down her neck, while his hand caressed her lower back, encouraging her even closer. Her gaze locked with his, and he couldn't resist her. He lowered his mouth to hers and gently covered her lips, searching and testing.

Being with her like this felt right—like coming home.

Dear Reader,

For Avery's story, I turned to an event from real life. My best friend Lori, executive director of The Hinsdale Humane Society, mentioned that the shelter owns their building, but the city of Hinsdale owns the land. While this has worked wonderfully for them since 1953, what if the situation suddenly changed? In *The Rancher and the Vet*, what if Avery's shelter thought they owned the land, but discovered they didn't when the owner's heirs decide to sell the property? Suddenly the shelter needs to raise a huge sum of money. Then to throw Avery further off balance I had her first love, Reed Montgomery, waltz back into town.

I'd come up with a tortured situation for Avery, and then I turned to Reed. I made him responsible for the well-being of a teenager—a teenage girl, no less! Being the only female in a household of five, I've learned men and women see the world differently. While that definitely makes life fun, it also causes problems, as Reed discovers with his niece. I hope you enjoy Avery and Reed's adventures.

Blessings, and remember—adopt, don't shop!

Julie

P.S. I love hearing from readers. Contact me at www.juliebenson.net.

The Rancher and the Vet

JULIE BENSON

HARLEQUIN® AMERICAN ROMANCE®

Recycling programs
for this product may
not exist in your area.

ISBN-13: 978-0-373-75452-6

THE RANCHER AND THE VET

Copyright © 2013 by Julie Benson

This edition published by arrangement with Harlequin Books S.A.

For questions and comments about the quality of this book,
please contact us at CustomerService@Harlequin.com.

® and TM are trademarks of Harlequin Enterprises Limited or its
corporate affiliates. Trademarks indicated with ® are registered in the
United States Patent and Trademark Office, the Canadian Trade Marks
Office and in other countries.

Printed in U.S.A.

ABOUT THE AUTHOR

An avid daydreamer since childhood, Julie always loved creating stories. After graduating from the University of Texas at Dallas with a degree in sociology, she worked as a case manager before having her children: three boys. Many years later she started pursuing a writing career to challenge her mind and save her sanity. Now she writes full-time in Dallas, where she lives with her husband, their sons, two lovable black dogs, two guinea pigs, a turtle and a fish. When she finds a little quiet time, which isn't often, she enjoys making jewelry and reading a good book.

Books by Julie Benson
HARLEQUIN AMERICAN ROMANCE

For Lori Halligan

Some friends are silver. Some are gold.
You're twenty-four karat. Thanks for always being there
for me.

And to Lori Goddard

Just for being you.

Special thanks to the staff and volunteers of
The Hinsdale Humane Society for putting up with me
being underfoot and answering all my questions. (Pam
and Mary Alex, thanks for the laughs during lunch!) For
all of you, it's clear your work isn't a job, it's a calling.

Thanks also to John Milano, one of the wonderful
regulars at Starbucks at Custer and Renner in
Richardson, for answering my legal questions and
helping out when I was at my wit's end.

Chapter One

"I'm being deployed to Afghanistan. I need you to come to Estes Park and take care of Jess."

Reed Montgomery straightened in his black leather desk chair with the lumbar support, his cell phone clutched in his now-sweaty hand as he processed what his older brother had said.

Colt was being deployed to Afghanistan. Soldiers went there and never returned.

Then the remainder of his brother's words sank in. *I need you to come to Estes Park and take care of Jess.*

He loved his niece, but the thought of being responsible for a child left Reed shaking. He didn't want children. The pressure. The fear of screwing up and damaging the kid for life. To top it off, taking care of any kid would be hard enough, but a teenage *girl?* That could send the strongest bachelor screaming into the night.

"Tell me I heard you wrong."

"I need you to watch Jess."

His brother had lost his mind.

Once Reed's brain kicked back into gear and his panic receded, he remembered his niece still had one set of grandparents. "I thought the plan was for Lynn's parents to stay with her."

"That was the idea, but when I called them I learned Joanne broke her hip last month and needed surgery."

"And they're just telling you now?"

"We don't talk much since Lynn died. They blame me for her death."

Almost a year ago, after fifteen years of marriage, Colt's wife had said she was sick of ranch life and had run off with her lover, only to die in a head-on collision a month later. Colt had picked up the pieces of his life, and explained as best he could to Jess that she hadn't been responsible for her mom leaving.

Lynn's death had also meant that Colt had to revise his family-care plan in case he was deployed.

"You weren't driving the car. Her lover was."

"They think if I'd been a better husband, she wouldn't have left. In their opinion I should've spent more time at home and less time with the reserves. Blaming me is easier than accepting the truth."

An only child, Lynn had grown up catered to— spoiled rotten, actually. Colt's wife had been high-maintenance, self-centered and had believed her husband's life should revolve around her.

"Is Joanne doing well enough that Jess could go live with them in Florida?" In addition to being unqualified for the job, Reed thought, his life and business were here in San Francisco. How could he up and leave for Colorado?

"She said she should be eventually, but there's another problem. Their retirement community only lets children stay for a week. Last night Herb brought up the subject at a town hall meeting, and everyone went crazy. The Association of Homeowners thinks if it makes an exception for Jess, within a month they'll be overrun with kids."

"Threaten them with a lawsuit. That'll make them back down. Better yet, give me your in-laws' number. I'll have my lawyer call them."

"You need their phone number, but there's no point in them talking to your lawyer." As Colt rattled off the phone number, Reed added it to his computer address book. "Even if they made an exception, Jess refuses to live in 'an old folks' neighborhood where people drive golf carts because they're scared to drive a car.' That's a direct quote. She said when she stays with her grandparents they never go anywhere. So in her words, she'd be a prisoner."

While he felt bad for his niece, that didn't mean Reed wanted to return to the old homestead and play dad. He'd been happy to see Estes Park in the rearview mirror of his beat-up truck when he left for Stanford. The thought of returning for anything longer than a weekend visit left him queasy.

"You're the parent. Don't ask Jess what she wants. Tell her what she's going to do."

Colt laughed. "That's easy to say for someone who doesn't have kids. I tried the strong-arm approach. She threatened to run away."

"Teenagers say that every time they don't get their way."

"I think she meant it, Reed." Colt's voice broke. "She's been having trouble since Lynn died, but she won't talk about it. Last year she started cutting classes and sneaking out at night to meet friends. Living in a retirement community and going to a new school would only make things worse."

Somehow Reed couldn't connect the sweet niece

he'd seen a year and a half ago at Christmas with the teenager his brother described. Jess had been eager to please, had loved school and was an excellent student. He stared at her picture on the corner of his mahogany desk. Her wide smile and twinkling brown eyes spoke of how carefree she'd been. Of course, the photo had been snapped before her mom ran off. He knew how that betrayal had affected Colt, but how could a kid wrap her head around something like that?

And his brother expected him to deal with a teenager who'd lost her mother and was acting out? What did he know about dealing with difficult children? Nothing except the piss poor example his father had given him. His stomach dropped. When Jess pushed him, and she would—hell, all teenagers did, even the good ones— how would he deal with it? Would he react like his old man, with a closed mind and an iron fist?

No, he was better than his father.

He'd worked hard to become the man he was today and, unlike his father, he tried to do something about his anger. When Reed had worried he might repeat the cycle of violence, he'd taken an anger-management class. Of course, going back to Estes Park and dealing with a teenager could test the techniques he'd learned.

The good news was he and Jess got along well. He loved his niece, and to her he was the cool uncle who sent great gifts like the newest iPhone. They'd be okay. "You really think she was serious about running away?"

"I wouldn't ask you to come here otherwise—not when you could be here up to a year. I know this will make running your business tough."

His cell phone beeped in his ear, alerting him to another call. Reed glanced at the screen. Damn. He'd been trying to get in touch with Phil Connor all morning.

Forcing himself to let the call go to voice mail, Reed focused on his brother's problem. "Tricky? Yes. Impossible? No. Could she come here instead?"

"As if dealing with losing her mom wasn't enough, soon after that her best friend moved to Chicago. Now I'm going to a war zone. I'm nervous about uprooting her, too. That's another reason I backed down when she balked about going to Florida. I need you to do this for me. You and Jess are the only family I've got."

The words hit Reed hard. He and Colt had always been close. Even before their parents died, he and Colt had relied on each other, sticking together through all the crap slung at them during childhood. While Reed's life the past few years had been almost perfect, Colt hadn't been as lucky. Life had knocked his brother around pretty well, especially the past year. How could Reed add to Colt's problems? Only a selfish bastard would say no.

"How soon do you need me there?"

"I leave in three days. If you get here tomorrow, that'll give us time to go over things before I leave." Colt's heavy sigh radiated over the phone lines. "If anything happens to me, promise me you'll—"

"Don't say that." While Reed tried to fill his voice with confidence, he knew there was no guarantee Colt would come home in one piece, or come home at all.

"I've got to and, dammit, Reed, you *will* listen. If I don't come back, promise me you'll watch out for Jess. Sure, Lynn's parents would take her, but I'm not sure that's best for her, especially if they won't move to Colorado."

"I give you my word, but you've got to take care. Don't do anything stupid. You don't have to be a superhero."

Colt chuckled, but the sound rang flat in Reed's ears. "Deal."

After ending his conversation with his brother, Reed returned Phil's call and reassured his client that their project was still on schedule. He was proud of his company, of what he'd accomplished. RJ Instruments was small, with only forty employees, but it was *his*. Something he'd created from nothing, and the company was holding its own in the market. They were the up-and-comers in the semiconductor business, making the chips that drove many of today's electronic wonder gadgets.

Of course, all of that could change when he started running things remotely.

Reed turned his attention to his calendar and his upcoming meetings. Some he could handle via Skype. With a laptop and his cell phone, he could run his business long-distance for a couple of months, but more than that? Probably not. His customers would want to see him in person. He'd have to make in-person sales calls to launch SiEtch. He smiled, thinking of their newest product. If he was right, they'd revolutionize the semiconductor industry, but they were approaching some crucial deadlines for release. He definitely couldn't run his business remotely for a whole year until Colt returned.

He hadn't gotten where he was by letting fate toss him around. He'd created a solid business by being proactive. His mind worked the problem, rehashing the immediate issues forcing him to return to Colorado— the Association of Homeowners' age restriction and Jess's resistance.

No matter what Colt thought, the first step was tackling the association's age restriction. Reed turned to his computer and clicked on his address book to locate

Colt's in-laws' number. Then he opened a new email,
hit the priority icon and typed a message to his lawyer.

Contact my brother's in-laws to get the contact information for their Association of Homeowners. I need
the association to make an exception for my niece to
stay with her grandparents indefinitely while Colt's in
Afghanistan. Threaten them with an age-discrimination
lawsuit. Do whatever you have to, but get the exception. Until I receive the approval, I'll be forced to relocate to Colorado to take care of my niece.

Reed hit Send and leaned back in his chair. Surely
when the exemption came through he could convince
Jess to see things his way, especially when staying with
her grandparents was best for her. There she'd have a
woman to talk to and two people who'd actually raised
a child, instead of an uncle who couldn't keep gold-
fish alive.

Next Reed called Ethan, his vice president of engineering, and asked him to come to his office. He'd met
Ethan fresh out of college when they'd started working
as software engineers at the same company. Eventually
Reed had moved to the management track while Ethan
pursued the technical route. The guy was a genius in
that area, and the first person Reed had hired when he
started RJ Instruments.

When Ethan arrived, Reed motioned toward the
black leather couch. Then he walked across his office
and settled into the wing chair to his friend's right. He
glanced up at the print of a hole at Pebble Beach on the
wall behind his sofa. Below the photo were the words
The harder the course, the more rewarding the triumph.
He hoped that held true this time.

"I need to update you on something that developed this morning." Reed explained about Colt's deployment and his leaving for Colorado.

"What about the customer calls you're scheduled to make next week?"

When clients had questions or needed hand-holding, Reed picked up the phone or hopped on a plane if necessary and handled the situations. While both he and Ethan understood the technology, over the past few years Ethan had developed issues dealing with some clients, becoming frustrated when they refused to see things his way. Now he'd have to step up and take on more of those responsibilities.

"I hope I can handle most of the issues with conference calls or on Skype. I might be able to pull off a quick day trip." Fly out, meet with the client and rush back to Colorado. Or he and Jess could leave Friday afternoon for a meeting/vacation trip. "But if those options don't work, you'll have to go instead."

"If I have to, I guess I have to."

"I can still run the weekly status meeting as usual via Skype. Between the two of us, we can reassure clients they won't see any difference in our service or attention to detail. We need to make sure everyone understands my being in Colorado won't affect our timelines, either, especially for SiEtch's release."

"I still think we're missing the mark, and we should lower our price point."

No way would he discuss that issue with Ethan again. They disagreed, and nothing either one said would change the other's mind. "My lawyer's working on getting approval for my niece to move in with her grandparents. Six months at the outside and I'll be back here running things."

Ethan shook his head, and chuckled. "I don't envy you. Six months with a teenage girl? I hope you can manage to stay sane."

"It shouldn't be too bad. School starts a couple of days after I get there. How hard can it be when she's gone eight hours a day?"

REED'S STOMACH KNOTTED up when Estes Park came into view. The main drag into town was four lanes now instead of two, but even at rush hour, the traffic seemed nonexistent by San Francisco standards and, damn, a turtle moved faster! They passed The Stanley Hotel, a white giant perched on a hill above the town. Farther down W. Elkhorn Avenue, shops catering to the tourists that kept the town of ten thousand alive lined the sidewalks. So many people came to Estes Park to enjoy the scenery, shop and relax. Here, they could get away from their lives and slow down for a while. Recharge their batteries.

Not Reed. How would he face anyone after what he'd done to his father? Sure, he'd changed, but everyone in Estes Park knew who he'd been. That's why when he visited Colt he stayed on the ranch, but that wouldn't be an option now.

As they left the town behind and drove past other bigger ranches, Reed longed to be back in the city where he could blend in with the masses. Where he could walk past people and no one knew him. No one knew what he'd spent a lifetime running from.

When Colt turned down the long gravel driveway to the Rocking M, Reed's chest tightened. Pine and aspen trees stood guard. Others would call the rustic ranch settled among the rugged Rocky Mountains beautiful, maybe even going so far as serene, but not

Reed. The mountains loomed over the ranch like silent giants, reminding him of his father—harsh, unyielding and domineering.

Memories bombarded him as the simple ranch house came into view. Colt had painted the place a soft brown instead of the dingy cream Reed remembered and had planted new landscaping, but the alterations couldn't change his memories or the fact that he'd been glad to be free of the place. For Reed, the old man's presence dominated everything on the ranch. Even after all these years and everything he'd done to shake him.

Like staying away from Estes Park while his father had been alive.

"You know where the guest room is," Colt said once they stepped inside the front door. "When you're ready I'll give you the rundown on the place."

While Reed had returned to the Rocking M since Colt owned the place, his visits had so far consisted of a Thanksgiving weekend or a couple of days over Christmas, and he'd avoided going into town. He'd worked so hard to leave his past behind, but that was hard to do when everyone in town knew who he'd been.

Especially Avery.

Ben McAlister, Avery's father, had done him a favor all those years ago, though at the time, Reed had thought it had been the worst thing ever to happen to him.

Your father's an alcoholic who beats the people he claims to love. You've changed this summer, and I hate to say it, but I see glimpses of him in you, son. You need to grow up and deal with your past. Until you do that, all you'll do is drag my daughter down with you.

As Reed trudged up the stairs he told himself he'd be damned if he'd let his memories pull him back.

He walked into the guest bedroom and his throat

closed up. While the room looked nothing like it had when he'd lived here—now resembling a hotel room with its nondescript accessories and earth tones—all he saw was the past. He pictured himself as a scared child, huddled in the corner between his bed and the wall as the sounds of his parents arguing shook the house. He remembered how often he curled up on his bed, his chest aching from the blows his father's meaty fists had delivered. He pictured himself as a teenager sprawled on the floor, the world spinning around him from drinking too much beer to numb the pain.

He'd never been able to stand being here for longer than four days. How would he handle staying for possibly a year? One nightmare at a time. And he'd do what he'd always done. He'd focus on work. After dumping his suitcase in the closet, he practically ran out of the room.

When he and Colt toured the ranch, Reed realized almost as many ghosts taunted him outside as in the damned house. They walked past the hay pasture and he remembered how his dad had smacked his head so hard his ears rang for a day after he'd gotten the tractor wheel stuck in a hole and it had taken them over an hour to pull the thing loose.

Don't go there. Remember who you are, not who you were.

He needed to remain focused on tasks and what needed to be done while Colt was gone. If he stayed busy enough he might survive. "I knew Dad sold some land before he died, but I didn't know it was this much."

"Damn near half of the acreage. My guess is once you left he was too lazy to do the work and too cheap to hire hands, so selling off the land and stock was the easiest way to keep a roof over his head and his liquor cabinet full."

"That sounds like our father."

"I've been rebuilding the place, but it's been slow going."

Especially with a wife like Lynn. Reed often thought if she hadn't gotten pregnant in Colt's senior year, she and his brother would've broken up after high school. Instead, his brother had graduated, enlisted in the air force and they got married.

Five years ago when their father died, Colt bought Reed's share of the ranch, and his family returned to Colorado. His brother hoped putting down roots would make his wife happy, since she'd grown weary of military life, something he loved. Something he saw as a calling. Part of the compromise had been that Colt could join the National Guard Reserves. Unfortunately, despite everything Colt did, he didn't get the happy ending.

Reed had gotten the better end of the deal. He'd used the money Colt paid him to start his company.

The dusty smell of hay hit him when they entered the barn, bringing with it reminders of the hours he'd spent toting hay and horse feed to the barn.

"How can you stand living here? Don't the memories get to you?"

"I just remember the bastard's dead and buried. I've had a damned good time changing things around the place. I hope some of them have him turning over in his grave. That gives me a whole helluva lot of pleasure." Colt thumped his brother on the back. "I know this is tough for you."

"I'll be honest. I'm not sure I can stand being here a

year." He looked his brother straight in the eyes. "You don't know what it was like after you left."

While they were teenagers, Colt had saved Reed more than once. When their dad went on a tirade, Reed shouted back or argued. He and his father went at it like two bulls stuck in the same pasture. Colt was the one who stepped in to defuse the situation, or he hauled Reed off before his dad could beat him to death. When Colt left for the air force, their father's anger had spiraled out of control.

He'd come home one night to find his dad drunk and spoiling for a fight, hammering on his favorite subject—how Reed was a bastard for leaving him to fend for himself. One thing led to another, and his father had punched him in the face. Something inside Reed had shattered that night, and without Colt there, he exploded.

He whirled, delivering blow after blow until his father collapsed on the floor. His chest heaving, Reed stood over the man who had tormented him for years. Then the reality of what he'd done sank in. He'd stooped to his father's level by taking his anger out on another human being. His father roused enough to scream that he'd make Reed pay. He'd call the police and see that Reed's sorry, ungrateful ass landed in jail.

Panic consuming him, Reed ran out of the house. Hours later, he found himself at the McAlisters' front door. Avery held him while the whole damned mess poured out of him. Then she'd woken up her parents.

Once Reed had explained to Avery's parents what had happened, Ben McAlister had called his lawyer. When Reed claimed he couldn't afford that, Ben told him not to worry about the money. Without Ben paying for his attorney, Reed could've gone to jail. He never knew the details of how Ben and his attorney got his father to drop the charges. They never said, and he never asked.

That one event had changed him in ways he still didn't understand.

"I've got an idea what it was like. That's why you coming back to stay with Jess was always the backup plan. That's why I didn't want to ask you to do it, and if Joanne hadn't broken her hip, I wouldn't have."

"I'm also worried about dealing with Jess." That and holding his company together, but Reed left out that detail. Colt carried enough weight on his shoulders.

When Reed had first spotted Jess at the airport, dressed in tight, low-cut jeans with a deep V-neck sparkly T-shirt that barely covered her midriff, he'd wanted to turn around and catch the first plane going anywhere.

"If I can't handle being here…if I get your in-laws' Association of Homeowners to make an exception, and I can get Jess to agree, are you okay with her living with her grandparents?"

Colt nodded. "As long as Jess agrees, I'm fine with it."

Reed's fear subsided now that he had a safety net.

"Jess is a good kid. Lynn's leaving really did a number on her. How the hell could she run off on her daughter? She didn't even have the nerve to tell Jess before she left. I had to," Colt said as they walked toward the horse stalls. "Damn, that was hard. You should've seen Jess's face. She looked at me with those big brown eyes of hers, and asked why her mom didn't love her anymore."

Reed stood there stunned. He knew Lynn's leaving had been bad, but Colt hadn't told him what a bitch she'd been. "You sure picked a winner."

"You're right about that. The only good thing I got

out of that marriage was Jess. She's worth whatever hell I went through." Colt shoved his hands into his jeans pockets. "School starts the day after tomorrow. It about takes a crowbar to get Jess out of bed, and she takes forever to get ready. Classes start at eight. If she isn't up by seven, she'll be late. You need to leave by seven forty-five."

Reed jotted down information about Jess's routines, the location of important documents and anything else he thought he might need to remember.

"She seems nervous about starting high school this year." Colt shook his head. "I don't remember us worrying about the kind of stuff she does—imagined slights, who's best friends with who, who said what about her outfit. The worst arguments are about boys. Girls are downright mean to each other. And their fights…" Colt whistled through his teeth.

"Worse than ours?"

Colt nodded as they walked past another stall. "We pounded on each other, but then it was over. Not with girls. When they get mad the emails and tweets fly. Girls divide into two camps. Then the tears start. Sometimes for days, and Jess won't talk about it. Then when I think it'll never end, they're all friends again."

Lord help him. He'd rather fight off a hostile takeover than face what Colt had just described. Why didn't society ship all teenage girls off to an island, and allow them to come back only once their sanity returned?

"You're not making me feel better about this. What do you do during all this drama?"

"Drama? That attitude will get you in trouble."

Reed froze as a lilting feminine voice washed over him. How many times had he heard that sultry voice in his dreams? Way too many to count, but never once when he'd come back had he sought her out. He wasn't one to borrow trouble. They were too different. He couldn't live here again, and she wouldn't live anywhere else. More important, though, she wanted children and he didn't.

He glanced over his shoulder at the woman coming out of a horse stall two doors down. She'd been pretty in high school, but the word failed to describe her now. Tall and willowy, even dressed in dirty jeans and a shapeless scrub top, without any makeup, the woman before him could stop traffic when she crossed the street.

Avery McAlister.

Staring at the beautiful blonde in front of him, he knew he'd been right to avoid Avery, because seeing the only woman he'd ever loved hurt worse than any blow he'd taken from his father.

Chapter Two

"Avery, what are you doing here?"

"It's good to see you, too, Reed." Avery laughed nervously as she forced herself to remain outwardly calm despite the blood pounding in her ears.

The last time she'd seen him he'd been tall and lanky, but in the years since, his frame had filled out in all the right ways. His shoulders were broader now, and he might even have grown an inch or two. His chiseled features, strong jaw and short black hair remained the same. Dressed in tailored slacks and a pinstriped shirt, Reed Montgomery, the boy she'd dated and fallen in love with in high school, had grown into a fine-looking man.

And he didn't show the slightest hint of guilt over breaking up with her via email all those years ago.

Avery tried to shut off the memories, but they broke free. She and Reed had met in Mrs. Hutchison's kindergarten class. They'd been seated at the same table and were busy drawing when Bennett Chambers yanked the yellow crayon from her hand. She'd been about to punch him in the arm when Reed whispered something she couldn't hear to Bennett. The boy's eyes widened and he paled, then a second later she had the yellow crayon.

They began dating their sophomore year of high school and fell in love soon after. In their senior year, Reed gave her a promise ring and they started making plans for their future. They both wanted to go to college. He'd received a scholarship from Stanford to study business, and she had one from Colorado State to study veterinary medicine, but he promised to come home as often as he could. Then a month after leaving for California, he sent her a short email. He loved living on the West Coast. He didn't want to come back to Colorado. Ever. He didn't want to get married. He didn't want children. He thought it was best they end things.

Being young, foolish and unable to let the relationship go that easily, Avery had called him. When he didn't answer, she'd left tearful messages on his voice mail, begging him to talk to her, which he never did. Then she wrote long letters that came back unopened.

Staring him down now, she reminded herself she wasn't the naive teenager willing to beg a man not to break up with her anymore, and she was damned if she'd let him see how much his coming back shook her.

"I'm here checking on Charger's injured foreleg. I'm a vet now, and the director of the Estes Park animal shelter." *Take that. I went on with my life and made something of myself.*

"I'm glad you're doing well, though I'm not surprised. You always could do anything you put your mind to."

Except hang on to you.

Their small talk sounded inane considering how intimate they'd once been. "What are you doing here, Reed?"

"I'm staying with Jess while Colt's in Afghanistan."

So that's what had brought him back. She turned to Colt. About the same height as his younger brother and almost as handsome, Colt had inherited their mother's blond hair while Reed resembled their dark-haired father. "I'll keep you and Jess in my prayers while you're gone."

Colt nodded. "I appreciate that."

"You're staying here for what, a year? Eighteen months?" she asked Reed. "You must have a very understanding boss."

"A year. Luckily I own my own small company, and thanks to Skype it shouldn't be too difficult to run things long-distance."

He was still as confident as ever, Avery mused, and yet she wondered if Reed's plan was one that looked great on paper, but wouldn't work well in practice.

"Wow. You own a company."

"It's not as glamorous as people think. I put in more hours than any of my employees, and I get a salary like everyone else. Most of what the company makes goes right back into developing new products."

A cell phone rang. "I'm sorry. I've got to take this call," Reed said.

As he moved away, his phone glued to his ear, Avery turned to Colt. "Are you sure about this? I think running a business long-distance will be harder than he thinks."

"I don't have a choice." Colt explained about his mother-in-law's health issues, the age restrictions in his in-laws' community and Jess's reluctance to live with her grandparents. "Reed will settle in. He'll do right by Jess."

Colt's daughter had gone through so much over the past year. Some women shouldn't have a pet, much less a child, and Lynn Montgomery had been one of those women. Now Jess's dad was being deployed. How much could a teenage girl take?

Avery wondered where she would've been without her mother to talk to during her adolescence. Her dad had been great, but he'd never quite understood things from her perspective. He saw things, well, like a *guy*. Did Jess have any women in her life to talk to now that her father was being deployed and she would be living with her bachelor uncle?

Who had never wanted children.

"Reed hasn't been around Jess very much. Are you sure he can handle this?"

She shook herself mentally. She always did this—got attached to any stray that wandered across her path. Colt was Jess's father. If he thought Reed was the best person to care for his child, who was she to criticize? But neither of them knew what it was like to be a teenage girl, one of the most insecure creatures on the planet.

Reed joined them, irritation marring his classic good looks. "Jess and I have a good relationship. We'll be fine. She's not an infant that needs watching 24/7. Things will be hectic for a while until I've reassured my customers that my physical absence won't affect my business, but then everything will settle into a predictable routine."

Avery laughed. "Predictable routine? With a teenager? Good luck with that."

"She has a point, Reed," Colt added. "Teenagers give mules stubborn lessons. You'll have to be a little flexible."

"Lucky for me I've got great negotiation skills."

"Good thing, because you'll need them." *Pride co-*

meth before the fall popped into Avery's mind. With Reed's attitude, one was sure coming. Not that it was her concern. Needing to steer the conversation to a safer topic, Avery said, "Charger's leg is better. I changed the dressing. The redness and swelling have subsided, but keep him away from the other horses a while longer. I don't want the wound getting reopened."

"How much do I owe you?"

Avery waved her hand through the air, dismissing the question. "Nothing. You didn't ask me to come by. I did that on my own. It's the least I can do. By the way, I wanted to remind you Thor is due for his annual shots."

"Thor?" Reed asked, knowing the shots would fall to him to get done.

"That's Jess's dog." Avery reached into her back pocket, pulled out a business card and handed it to Reed. "Call the office and set up an appointment."

"When did Jess get a dog?" Reed asked his brother.

"Must've been a couple of months after the last time you were here."

"The fact that you didn't know Jess has a dog says a lot about your relationship. I bet you're one of those uncles who sends birthday and Christmas gifts, but can't bother with anything else. If that's the case, you're in for a bumpy ride." With that, Avery turned and hurried out of the barn. Reed Montgomery was back, and worse yet, he could still make her heart skip a beat.

WHEN AVERY WALKED INTO the shelter twenty minutes later to a chorus of barking and meows, she still hadn't regained her emotional balance from seeing Reed. When she'd first spotted him, her palms had grown sweaty. Her heart had raced. All reactions she hadn't experienced with a man in far too long.

She needed to go on a date with someone. Anyone. What had it been? Six months? Longer? That was her problem. She'd been neglecting her social life.

Like that was something new?

When she found time to date, it seemed no one could hold her interest. Invariably she discovered some irritating habit she couldn't overlook, or her boyfriend's future plans conflicted with hers. Whatever the reason, the fun and attraction fizzled out after a few months.

Stop it. Focus on work and quit thinking about Reed and your pathetic love life.

So far the week had been a good one for the shelter. Five dogs, six cats and three horses had been adopted. They'd gotten enough donations to buy animal food to last until the end of the next month. Hopefully the recent events indicated an upward trend.

"Betty Hartman called this morning and said she couldn't come in," Emma Jean Donovan, Avery's volunteer coordinator and right-hand gal, said the minute Avery walked into the front reception area.

"Oh, the joys of working with volunteers." People thought nothing of canceling at the last minute, not realizing how the shelter relied on them to accomplish many of the daily tasks, chores that had to be done, no matter what.

"Because she wasn't here, Shirley didn't have anyone to gossip with, so guess who got an earful?"

"Better you than me, Em."

"All she could talk about was Reed Montgomery being back in town."

"So I discovered when I stopped by the Rocking M this morning."

"You *saw* him? Are you okay?"

While Em had been two years behind Avery and

Reed in school, everyone in town knew about their messy breakup. The news had spread through Estes Park High faster than the flu. "I was barely eighteen when we broke up. I got over him ages ago. So what if he's back? I don't care."

"Oka-a-ay." Em drew out the word, and tossed her a sly whatever-you-say-though-I-don't-believe-a-word-of-it grin. "You don't have to convince me. Is he still hot?"

"He looked sort of silly standing there in the barn wearing dress pants and a pinstriped shirt, but I guess he's attractive in a California yuppie sort of way."

Liar. He'd looked better than ever. He'd been a teenager when he left. He was all man now.

"I could get used to California yuppie. If you're not interested, do you mind if I make a play for him?"

"He probably has a yuppie girlfriend, but if he doesn't, go for it." Annoyed with the topic and her internal hell-no reaction to Em's question, Avery steered the conversation back to shelter business. "Has anything happened that I actually *need* to know about?"

"We had an abandoned mama dog and her litter dropped off this morning. The pups are about three weeks old."

So much for the to-do list she'd compiled last night. Avery's top priority now became examining the latest arrivals and getting them ready for foster care. The commotion at the shelter was too much for a mama and her babies, especially for the five weeks until they could be put up for adoption. "Got any ideas of who can foster the little family?"

"It's already taken care of. Jenny will pick them up once you give them the all clear."

"You're amazing."

"And on only four hours' sleep."

"I heard the band was playing at Halligan's. How'd the gig go?"

Music and her country-and-western band were Emma's first loves, with animals a close second. She worked at the shelter to pay her bills, and moonlighted playing at area bars in the hopes that someone would spot her and offer her a record deal.

Emma's face lit up. "The crowd was small but enthusiastic. My new song went over well."

"When your record deal comes through, promise me you'll train someone before you leave me. Not that anyone would do the job as well as you do, but at least then I'll have a chance for survival."

"I am one of a kind." A beaming Emma held out an envelope. "This came by registered mail."

Avery read the return address. Franklin, Parker and Simmons, attorneys at law in Denver. "Let's hope it's good news. Maybe someone left us a bequest in their will."

She tore open the envelope, pulled out the letter and started reading. The missive indeed dealt with a will— Sam Weston's. Twenty-five years ago, when Geraldine Griswald had created an animal shelter, her husband and Sam were hunting buddies. Sam, also an animal lover, rented Geraldine a piece of land with a tiny building along Highway 35 East for one dollar a year. Eventually, the shelter raised money and built a bigger facility.

Avery read further. No. This couldn't be right. The shelter didn't own the land their building stood on? Everyone believed Sam had donated the land to the Estes Park animal shelter over fifteen years ago.

This couldn't be happening.

She read further. Sam's heirs wanted to sell all his

land to a developer, including the parcel where the shelter stood. They'd "generously" offered to let the shelter buy their lot if they matched the developer's price of three hundred thousand dollars. Otherwise, they had forty-five days to move.

Three hundred thousand dollars. Just raising a 20-percent down payment of sixty grand would be daunting in the allotted time. Avery swallowed hard and tried to push down her panic.

The Estes Park animal shelter was the only one for miles. If it closed, the other shelters would have trouble dealing with the additional demands on their resources, and the animals would pay the price.

"From the look on your face, I'm guessing it's bad news."

Talk about an understatement, but Avery couldn't tell Emma that. Until she checked into the situation, she'd keep the news to herself. But if she discovered they didn't own the land, everyone would hear about the situation, because they'd need every cent they could get to keep the shelter open.

"Nothing I can't handle." Avery inwardly winced. How could she say that with a straight face, especially to Emma who knew her so well? They'd both pinched every penny thin over the past few months to keep the shelter afloat, but she thought she could come up with sixty grand? Delusional, that's what she was.

"Next thing you'll try to sell me the Rocky Mountains."

So much for keeping the news to herself, because she refused to lie to Emma. Glancing around the front room, Avery made sure no volunteers or other staff members were around before she told Emma the news.

"What are we going to do? Do I need to update my résumé?"

"Don't you dare. I need your help now more than ever. This is the game plan. While I'm examining the new arrivals, you'll contact the property clerk to find out who they show owns the land."

"What about the board?"

Avery cringed. Harper Stinson, the shelter's board president and a top graduate from the micromanager school of business, had hinted they could solve all their financial problems by cutting staff. If Avery didn't handle the situation carefully, Harper would run amok through the streets of Estes Park with the news of the shelter's impending doom.

"I'll figure out how to tell the board when I have more information." She'd be proactive. Assess the situation and develop a plan before she spoke to them.

"Lucky you."

"The board may be a big help. They've got a wide range of skills and talents, and that's exactly what we need right now."

"When they aren't arguing over who has the best idea and who should be in charge of the project." Emma shuddered. "I still have nightmares about our last dog-washing fund-raiser."

"Thanks for reminding me about that." Three of the board members had taken on organizing key aspects of the fund-raiser. Avery had been forced into the peacemaker role when the lines between the jobs blurred and toes got stepped on. "They'll pull together better this time because it's such a dire situation. You'll see."

"You're such an optimist."

"If I wasn't I'd never survive running a nonprofit agency."

REED'S DAY STARTED at the bank getting the forms notarized for him to be Jess's guardian while Colt was overseas. Then he and Jess took Colt to the airport. On the drive to Denver, his niece slouched in the backseat texting and ignored her dad's attempts at conversation, while Reed tried to ignore how much Jess's actions hurt Colt.

When Colt hugged Jess, telling her how much he loved her, and how he'd miss her, Reed's eyes teared up. He and his brother shook hands, thumped each other on the back, and Reed reminded Colt not to act like an idiot and get himself hurt. Then he prayed this wasn't the last time he would see his brother.

On the return trip, Jess sat stoically in the passenger seat, texting. After a few feeble efforts at conversation, she snapped that she didn't want to talk. Then she popped in earphones, cranked up her music and shut her eyes.

When they returned to the ranch, she retreated to her bedroom while Reed saw to the stock. A couple of hours later, dripping in sweat, muscles he hadn't used in years sore from hauling hay and water, he crawled into the shower.

After cleaning up, he headed downstairs to work on dinner. He'd learned to cook out of necessity when he and some college buddies lived off campus his senior year. Unable to afford eating out every day and sick of boxed mac and cheese, he'd turned to the internet and the Food Network.

He glanced at his watch. Not even six and he felt as though it was after midnight. As Reed added chopped garlic, onions and ginger to the chicken breasts cooking in the skillet, the aromas engulfed him. Though the sleek stainless-steel-and-earth-toned kitchen looked nothing like the one he remembered growing up, he still could see his mom standing in the same spot as he did now.

Life had been so different before she died of breast cancer.

He often wondered why she had married his father. Talk about opposites. His mom loved to cuddle up with her sons every night before bed and read to them. He could still hear bits and pieces of *Green Eggs and Ham* read in her soothing voice. His mom quickly and generously offered support and encouragement, while his father tossed out criticism and orders. When his temper exploded at his sons, his mom stepped in and smoothed things over or took the blows. She also kept his father's drinking in check. All that changed when she died.

Reed tossed sliced carrots, snap peas, broccoli and soy sauce in the pan. Nothing he'd ever done had been good enough for his father. When he showed an interest in business and computers, his father took that as a personal rejection. Ranching had been good enough for Aaron Montgomery and his father before him—why the hell wasn't that good enough for Reed? His father expected, no *felt,* his sons owed it to him to stay at the ranch and take care of him in his old age.

As if either he or Colt would do that after the hell their father put them through.

After plating the chicken and sautéed vegetables, he walked to Jess's room and knocked on the door. High-pitched barking sounded from inside. "Dinner's ready."

The door opened, and Jess stood there, a brown Chihuahua clutched to her chest. The dog immediately growled at him. "This is Thor?"

"What's wrong with my dog?" Jess asked, her voice laced with distrust and irritation.

Did all teenage girls twist the simplest questions into knots?

"When your dad told me you had a dog named Thor, this wasn't the image that came to mind." He'd envisioned a border collie or a shepherd mix. A dog that would be useful around a ranch, not one that fitted in a girl's purse. "Why'd you name him Thor? Don't girls usually name their dogs Mr. Boots or Prince Charming?"

"And you know that because you're such an expert?" Still clutching the dog, she stalked past him toward the kitchen.

He still couldn't get over the difference in his niece's appearance since he'd seen her last. With her dark brown shoulder-length hair and wearing enough makeup to start her own makeup counter, she was fourteen going on twenty-two.

When he reached the kitchen, Jess was seated at the round oak table, her dog settled on her lap. He was having dinner with his niece and her dog. Dogs belonged under the table begging for scraps, not seated on someone's lap. He opened his mouth to tell her to put Thor down, but paused. A fire burned in her eyes, as if she dared him to say something, as if she was spoiling for a fight. He'd entered labor negotiations where people looked at him with less animosity. A smart businessman picked his battles carefully.

Reed reached for the plate of chicken. The dog peered over the table and snarled.

"Does he growl at everyone, or is it just me he doesn't like?"

"He's very sensitive." Jess picked up a small piece of chicken and fed the morsel to her pet. "In his head, you came and Dad left. It's kind of a cause-and-effect thing."

"You sure it's okay for him to be eating chicken with soy sauce and all those spices?"

Jess rolled her eyes and made a tsking sound with her tongue as though she was the Dog Whisperer and he the idiot who couldn't spell *dog*.

This charged silence couldn't continue between them. Even he could tell she was bottling up her emotions, and anger simmered barely below the surface. Better to bring things out in the open than have them explode later, but how?

"What about you? What are your thoughts?" Reed kept his voice level and unconcerned.

"It's not like I had any choice."

"When I was your age, not having any say about something ticked me off big-time." Not that his father had ever noticed. Or would've cared if he had.

Jess shrugged and handed her dog another bite of chicken.

This was getting him nowhere. Could he use a strategy he applied to employees with Jess? Build a team atmosphere? "I know this is hard for you, and I've got to admit, it's not easy for me, either. Since Mom died when Colt and I were a little younger than you are now, we grew up in an all-male household, but I'm not that bad a guy, am I?"

Jess eyed him cautiously. "I don't know. The last time you were here, you left the toilet seat up. That really ticks a woman off, you know."

The chip Jess carried around on her shoulder had to be getting heavy. Maybe if he made her laugh, she'd loosen up. "In a show of good faith I'll invest in one of those toilets that have an automatic seat-lowering feature."

His niece smiled, ever so slightly. "Whatever."

"I wouldn't want to have to call your dad and tell him you fell into the toilet."

"Eww! Thanks for putting that image in my head!"

Her bright giggle thrilled him, easing the tightness in his chest. Maybe they could make a go of this. At least long enough for him to change her mind about staying with her grandparents. "I haven't worked on a ranch since I went to college." He'd gone to summer school to avoid coming back. "I'll be relying on you a lot."

Her smile faded, and her chocolate eyes darkened. "If you think I'm going to do all the work around here, forget it."

"I was thinking of you as an expert consultant." Giving someone a title helped an employee feel vested in a project. She nodded, but remained quiet. "Do I have any redeeming qualities, or am I a total pain in the ass?"

As Jess eyed him he could practically see the biting comment forming in her mind. Then her gaze softened. "You're a good cook. Even better than Dad, so at least we won't starve."

It wasn't much, but it was something.

THE NEXT MORNING AT FIVE Reed dragged himself out of bed, threw on jeans and a T-shirt and headed for the barn. He went to the hayloft and grabbed a bale, jumping when a rat scurried over his boots. At least it wasn't a snake. He'd never gotten used to them. What was the rule about which ones were poisonous? Something about red, black and yellow being a friend of Jack or killing a fellow, but that's all he recalled. Making a mental note to check Google for poisonous-snake sayings for future reference, he tossed the hay out of the loft.

While his muscles strained against the unfamiliar work, part of him had come to enjoy the physical exertion. The upside was he collapsed into bed at night exhausted enough that being back in his old bedroom didn't prevent him from falling asleep. Of course, he didn't sleep all that well, either, but one out of two wasn't bad.

He filled the hay bins in the stalls, then gave each horse some grain and fresh water. Next he went in search of a saddle, surprised to find his old one in the tack room. He smiled, remembering how he'd saved for a year to buy it. He ran his hand over the suede seat and the basket-weave tooling, then lifted the saddle and carried it into the stall of a calm chestnut. His body went into autopilot, his hands efficiently accomplishing the task of saddling the horse.

He rubbed the horse's neck. "Go easy on me. It's been a while since I've done any riding." Then hauled himself onto the animal. The old leather creaked under his weight. His heels tapped the horse's flanks, and the animal responded. So far so good. He was in the saddle, not on his ass in the hay.

As he made his way across the ranch toward the cow pasture, Reed settled into a rhythm with the horse. The stiffness he'd woken up with from tossing and turning most of the night eased with his movements. Colt had told him to keep a close eye on the cows. For a small herd, Colt said, they caused a surprising amount of trouble. Most of which revolved around finding holes in the fencing and traveling to Sam Logan's land.

The soft summer breeze teased his skin. The house disappeared from view, and he relaxed. Urging the horse into a gallop, he felt the tension drain from his body. He'd forgotten how freeing it felt to be on top of a magnificent animal riding hell-for-leather to nowhere in particular. Just running.

Recalling how often he and Avery had ventured into the national park to get away and just be together, he smiled. They'd ride and then stop near a mountain stream to talk and make out. There he'd been happy. At least until he returned home.

The herd came into view, thankfully still where they belonged. After a quick check of the fences Reed returned to the house, showered and then headed for Colt's office, where he pulled up an email from his lawyer.

He had a problem. According to his attorney, there was some federal act that let communities set age restrictions as long as they met certain criteria, like 80 percent of the houses having someone over fifty-five in residence. As long as they maintained that, the neighborhood could keep kids from living there.

After firing back instructions for his lawyer to check into the community's compliance, Reed glanced at his watch. Seven in the morning, and he hadn't heard Jess stirring. If she didn't get moving soon, they'd never make it out the door on time, and he'd start his day behind.

When he stepped into the hallway that led to the bedrooms, an alarm clock's irritating beep greeted him. How could she sleep through that?

He knocked on her door. Nothing. He knocked harder. "Jess? Are you awake?"

High-pitched yips masquerading as barking came from behind the door, but nothing from his niece. Now what? He sure as hell wasn't going in her room. Then, between the alarm beeps, he heard snoring. He pounded on the door. "Jessica! Shut off your blasted alarm, and get your butt out of bed!"

More yipping, followed by "All right!"

He glanced at his watch. "I'll expect you downstairs

for breakfast in twenty minutes. That will give you ten minutes to eat and brush your teeth, leaving five minutes to gather what you need for school before we head out."

He heard her shuffling around the room before the door flew open and he faced a scowling Jess dressed in boxer shorts and an oversize T-shirt. "You worked out how much time I need to brush my teeth and gather my stuff?"

"What's wrong with a schedule?"

"Nothing if you're the TV Guide Channel." She brushed her bangs out of her face. "Don't get your shorts in a wad. I've got plenty of time. They won't count me late on the first day."

He hadn't given a thought to the school counting her tardy. "We've got to leave by seven forty-five. I have an eight-thirty conference call." Also, he refused to set up bad habits. Managing his staff had taught him it was easier to create good patterns than to break poor ones.

"That's not *my* problem. I'll be down when I'm good and ready." She slammed the door in his face.

At seven-fifty he called his assistant to push back his conference call. He and Jess left at seven fifty-five.

When he returned to the house at eight-thirty, he opened the front door, stepped inside and slipped, nearly ending up on his backside.

Glancing down, he discovered puddles—and they weren't pee—dotting the wooden floor. As he stared at the trail heading upstairs toward the bedrooms, he wondered if he'd shut his door.

"Thor, you better not have gone in my room, or you'll be in trouble." *I'm threatening a dog. Three days with Jess and I'm going crazy.*

He followed the trail right to his open bedroom door.

Peering in, he discovered the damned dog sleeping on his pillow, away from the mess he'd created on the rest of the bed. "You're out to get me, aren't you?"

Not wanting to put off his conference call a second time, he made his way through the minefield to Colt's office, shut the door behind him and decided to deal with it all later. He spent the next hour reassuring clients that his being in Colorado wouldn't affect their business, while pretending his life hadn't become an exercise in surviving teenage angst and cleaning up after a vindictive Chihuahua.

After ending his call, he found rubber gloves, paper towels and a bucket to tackle Thor's messes. He'd muck out an entire barn before he'd pull this duty again. Any repeat incidents and he was calling in a hazmat team.

Next he retrieved Avery's business card from his wallet and punched in her number. As he waited for her to answer, he stormed into Jess's room.

Didn't every girl with a Chihuahua have a carrier-purse thing? Clothes covered the floor, making it look like a patchwork quilt made by a color-blind quilter. He scanned the disaster zone. If she had something to put the dog in, he'd spend the better part of the day finding it.

No way was he letting the little monster ride in Colt's truck unconfined. Some things were sacred, and a man's truck was in the top two. He headed for the kitchen to find a substitute carrier as Avery's voice answering the phone floated over him.

"I need your help."

Chapter Three

"Jess's dog has the runs." Reed walked into the kitchen. He glanced around the room. What could he use? "Can I bring him in?"

He flung open cabinet doors, searching. The plastic containers he found were too small, and Thor could get out without a lid. Then he spotted cloth grocery sacks hanging on the pantry door. He smiled and snatched one up.

"Thor's sick? Bring him in. On Thursdays we don't open until noon, but I'm going in early to do paperwork. I'll meet you at the shelter in twenty minutes."

Sack in hand, he thanked Avery, said he was on his way and returned to his bedroom. Maybe he'd get lucky and she'd keep the dog for a couple of days.

When Reed walked into the room, Thor eyed him suspiciously. Reed inched closer to the bed, trying to appear casual. The dog sat up and growled. Reed strolled to the dresser, opened a drawer and dug around inside.

I'm trying to carry off a sneak attack on a dog. I'm not going *crazy. I'm there.*

He stalked toward the dog, and Thor bolted under the bed.

Damn. No way was he getting on the floor to catch

the mutt. Instead he returned to the kitchen. When he looked inside the fridge he found deli ham. He stormed back to the bedroom, tore off a chunk and dropped the treat on the floor beside the bed. Seconds later, a little brown head appeared and gobbled up the meat. Reed tossed down another piece, this one farther away. Two tries later, he snatched up the dog, dumped him in the cloth bag and looped the handles through each other so Thor couldn't hop out, leaving enough of an opening for air to flow.

As he left the house, he realized fate seemed determined to throw him and Avery together. What were the powers that be trying to tell him? He shook his head. He didn't care. All he wanted to know was how to get them to leave him alone.

AVERY STOPPED AT THE FRONT DESK to locate Thor's file, and giggled thinking of Reed dealing with a Chihuahua with the runs. When she opened the door for him five minutes later, irritation darkened his handsome features.

"Where's Thor?" Then she noticed the black cloth grocery bag dangling from his large hands. Hands that knew her body well. No. She couldn't think about that. Focusing on the sack, she saw it move. She bit her lip, trying to hold in her laughter, but failed. "You put him in a grocery sack?"

"Woman, I've been pushed about as far as a man can be. You're taking your life in your hands, laughing." The minute he started speaking the dog growled. Reed glared at the bag. "And you better be nice to me after the bomb you dropped on my bed."

"He didn't."

"He sure as hell did, and all over the wooden floors."

The absolute horror on his face made her laugh harder. "I'm sorry. Really I am." She giggled one last time thinking of his reaction when he'd found his bed. It was amazing the dog was alive.

"It's funny to you because it wasn't your bed."

"Bring him in." She stepped aside for him to enter, and Reed's musky cologne tickled her senses. As he handed her the sack, she remembered how his scent clung to her clothes after they'd been necking, which led to images of the two of them together and a sudden spike in her heart rate.

Stop it. Trips down nostalgia lane led nowhere but back. She was all about moving forward with her life, and hoped she'd find someone who wanted the same things she did—a loving marriage and raising their children in the same town where she'd grown up. Something that Reed never would do.

"After I examine Thor, I'll let you know what's going on." For a minute she stood there, the silence between them shouting volumes.

He shifted his weight from one foot to the other. "This is awkward, isn't it?"

"I don't know what you expect me to say. I wasn't the one who ended things between us."

She'd told herself she'd gotten over him. But until she'd seen Reed in the barn the other day, she hadn't realized how much anger she still carried. They'd made love the first and only time the July after graduation. She'd loved him so much, wanted to spend the rest of her life with him, and then the relationship was over.

"We'd talked about our future so much, and never once did you mention the fact that you didn't want children. How could you have left out that important detail?" Giving voice to her anger and throwing the words in his face felt good. Closure. She finally had what she'd never known she craved.

"I don't know what to say other than I was young. When I got to college, I started thinking about what us having a future meant in practical terms, and it hit me."

"You gave me a promise ring, and then you never came back."

"I couldn't. Once I got away, I felt free. I didn't want to lose that, but you're right. I should've called you."

But it had been worse than that. She'd left messages begging for him to talk to her. Ones that he'd never returned.

Let it go.

"I was an ass, and I'm sorry I hurt you." He stepped toward her, then froze, as if he wasn't sure of what to do next. "Can we start over with a clean slate? Be friends?"

Friends? The word shouldn't have stung her pride, but it did.

Avery nodded. That would make things easier when they ran into each other, and in a town of less than ten thousand people, their paths would cross. "I'll call you when I know what's going on with Thor."

Dismissing Reed, Avery reached into the sack, lifted Thor out and snuggled with him for a minute. She waited for the sound of the door opening and closing as Reed left, but after a moment she glanced over her shoulder, finding him still standing there. "Is there something else you need?"

A familiar look flashed in his cobalt eyes as his gaze locked with hers. Her heart fluttered. Was he thinking the same thing she was? How much they'd once thought they needed each other?

"Jess will be worried when I tell her about Thor. Can I bring her by after school?"

"Absolutely. Chances are it's nothing serious, and he'll probably be ready to go home by then."

Reed nodded and then turned and walked out of the exam room. When she'd said they could start over, she'd thought doing so would make things easier. Then she'd asked him if he needed anything else, and now she wasn't so sure. The look she'd glimpsed in his eyes moments earlier was the same one she'd seen years ago, right before he kissed her.

LATER THAT AFTERNOON, as Reed sat in the pickup lane at Jess's school, his thoughts returned to Avery. He was thankful that they'd cleared the air. In a town the size of Estes Park, they'd run into each other. Now maybe things wouldn't be as awkward.

Who was he kidding? Things would still be awkward. Everything he'd loved about Avery—her giving spirit, her quiet strength, her down-to-earth nature— was still there, but there was something more now. Something more refined. Her appeal had heightened over the years. She was one of the most beautiful women he'd ever seen, and yet she seemed unaware of the fact.

The truck's passenger door opened, a red backpack flew behind the seat. Jess slid in, the leather seat squeaking with her movements. He tossed out the obligatory "How was your day?" and she responded with the typical teenage response of "Fine."

"I took Thor to the vet. He wasn't feeling well. I came home to messes all over the house."

Her eyes widened, and her lip quivered. "What's wrong? Is he okay? What did Dr. McAlister say? Is he home?"

The more questions Jess asked, the higher her voice

rose. He rushed to reassure her. "Avery—Dr. McAlister—said it probably wasn't serious, but she was going to run some tests. I said we'd stop by after school to check on him."

Minutes later, at the shelter, Avery walked into the exam room, Thor snuggled in her arms. Jess raced toward them.

"We gave this guy some fluids because he was a little dehydrated, but that's nothing to worry about, Jess," Avery commented in a soothing tone as she placed Thor on the metal table. "I ran some tests, but didn't find anything."

"Then why'd he get sick?"

Avery shrugged. "He might have eaten a plant or something outside that upset his system. Who knows. To help with the diarrhea I want you to give him some medicine once a day. The front desk will give you the dosage information when you check out."

Reed bit his lip to keep from saying he'd told Jess she shouldn't have given her dog the chicken last night, but he did toss a knowing glance in her direction.

"Let me show you both how to give Thor the medicine." Avery reached into her scrub-top pocket and pulled out a plastic syringe filled with the pink liquid. When Reed remained nailed to his seat, both she and Jess turned to him. "I can see fine from here. I'm responsible for Jess. She's responsible for the dog. That's the chain of command."

Jess shook her head and faced Avery. "He doesn't like Thor."

"The dog doesn't like me," Reed countered. As if to prove the point, Thor peered around Jess, glared at Reed and growled. "See."

"That's actually natural. Chihuahuas bond strongly

with their owners and tend to distrust people they don't know. Isn't that right, Thor?"

Reed frowned. The danged mutt wagged his tail. But then, what male wouldn't be hypnotized into submission receiving Avery's full attention?

"Thor doesn't understand why Colt is gone and you're here," Avery continued. "That adds to his uncertainty, but Jess can help him accept you."

Acceptance? All he wanted was the dog to stay out of his way, and do his business outside. He could live with distant disdain.

Avery glanced between Reed and his niece. "Jess, would you go to the front desk and get some dog treats so we can work with Thor?"

When the door shut behind the teenager, Avery faced Reed, her hands on her hips. "Did it ever occur to you that Thor is upset with you because he senses the tension between you and Jess?"

"I love my niece."

"Then prove it. You need to get to know her as a person. You need to show an interest in her life."

Reed stiffened. "That's going to take time. I just got here."

"Remember she's your niece, not one of your employees. And FYI, a good start would be making an effort to get along with her dog."

Before he could answer, his cell phone rang. He glanced at the screen and answered the call without so much as an *Excuse me.*

"What's up, Ethan?"

Avery shoved her hands into her lab-coat pockets and took a deep breath. "Get off the phone. My time is valuable. I've got other animals waiting."

Reed ended his call with a terse "I'll call you back."

The exam-room door swung open and Jess returned with the treats. The teenager glanced between the two adults. "Jeez, you two look like you're about to take a swing at each other. What did I miss?"

Was that how they looked? Reed paled and stepped back.

"It's nothing. Just a difference of opinion." Avery cleared her throat. "Jess, if you want to help Thor accept your uncle, he should take over caring for him for a couple of days."

"I don't know." Jess clutched her dog against her chest. "I want them to get along, but he's my dog."

"I understand. We can still do some things that will help." She asked the teenager to sit in a chair by the door while she worked with Reed. "Both of you need to reinforce Thor's good behavior with praise and treats, while you ignore the negative. Let me give you an example. Jess, if you're holding Thor and he growls at your uncle, put him down and turn your back. If he doesn't growl or act aggressively, Reed, you need to give him a treat and praise him in a high-pitched voice." She demonstrated. "We call it a Minnie Mouse voice."

"You've got to be kidding." Reed shook his head. "You're determined to crush my ego today, aren't you?"

"Like yours can't take the hit?" Avery teased.

"I'm willing to try if you are, Uncle Reed. Then you could help me give him his medicine."

For a moment, despite the dark eyeliner, Jess's wide brown eyes filled with innocence and she looked her age. How the hell could he say no to her when she looked at him like that? Had he ever been that innocent or trusting? Even before his mother died? "We'll give it a shot."

Avery spent the next couple of minutes working with

him and the dog. At one point he looked at Avery and said, "Thor's not the only one who needs reinforcement for positive behavior. I want some props for my effort here."

"Good job, Reed." Avery tossed the words out in a high, squeaky voice.

"That wasn't what I had in mind."

"Too bad. That's all you're getting." Their light banter reminded him of how comfortable he'd always felt with Avery. He'd been in love with her for dozens of reasons, one being how at ease he felt with her, but that was before he damn near beat his dad to death. Before he'd talked to her father and realized he loved her so much he had to let her go because she deserved better than he could give her.

Being back here still wasn't good for him, and she refused to live anywhere else. His thoughts stopped him cold. "I've got the idea. Jess and I can work on this at home." Before Avery could say anything, his cell phone rang again. "We done here?"

Avery nodded, handed the dog to Jess and headed out of the room. He answered the call and told the client he'd call back in five minutes. Then he joined Avery and Jess at the front desk. Reed scanned the bill, amazed that the charges were bigger than the dog.

"Avery, what's this I hear about the shelter not owning the land our building resides on?" The sparkle disappeared from Avery's gaze, and she stiffened as though someone had tied a broom handle to her back. Reed turned to see a woman with short salt-and-pepper hair dressed in jeans and a T-shirt with an elk on the front stride toward them.

Avery made the introductions. "Reed, Jess, this is Harper Stinson, the shelter's board president."

Years ago, when he'd been on the board of his boss's pet charity, Reed had learned a lot about the people who served on them. Some were crusaders. Others were out to make community business connections. Others still were bored housewives looking to find purpose. But no matter who they were, everyone had an agenda. What was this woman's?

"So, you're the Reed Montgomery that has everyone in town talking. I want you to know I'm keeping your family in my thoughts and prayers," Harper said. "We'll all be glad when your brother's back home safe and sound."

No one more so than him.

Jess tossed him a let's-go look. "Thor and I will wait outside."

As the door swooshed open and thunked close with Jess's exit, Reed glanced at Avery. "I appreciate you working Thor in this morning. I hope you got some paperwork done after I left."

When he turned to leave, Harper partially blocked his exit. "Since you brought up the topic of paperwork, Avery and I are developing a new business plan for the shelter. What do you think—"

"Reed's a busy man. He doesn't have time for shelter business," Avery insisted.

Her stiff posture and the way she nibbled on her lower lip told him Avery had reached her patience limit. Something was going on between these two. Any businessperson worth two cents knew better than to discuss their business in public, especially in front of strangers.

"Avery's right about that. I've got my hands full with Jess and my own company."

"Our main sticking point is staffing issues," Harper continued, completely ignoring his and Avery's comments. "I'm sure you know that while no one likes to cut staff, sometimes it's necessary to lower operating costs."

Now he knew her agenda. Harper wanted him to back her up against Avery. "I've found people often latch onto that solution because it's easier than working to find other ones," he said.

He glanced at Avery and found her eyes shining with gratitude. When she smiled, his insides twisted, and he swore his chest puffed out.

Avery flashed him a tight smile. "Reed needs to go, since Jess is waiting for him. I'm sure she has homework to do. If you have any other problems with Thor, call me."

As he left he almost pitied Harper. He'd seen that look in Avery's eyes today, and unless he missed his guess, Harper was in for a stinging lecture on business etiquette.

As Avery ushered Harper into her office, she struggled to control her temper. How dare she burst into the shelter and take her to task in front of Reed and Jess? Worse yet, she'd tried to pull Reed into their disagreement and use him to get her to knuckle under.

As Avery sank into her worn desk chair, it squeaked under her movement. Before she could explain her position, Harper said, "Why wasn't I informed the minute you received word from Sam Weston's lawyers?"

"I wanted to research our options before talking to you." Avery placed her folded hands on her desk. When her fingers started tingling, she loosened her grip. "If you need to talk to me about shelter issues, especially our disagreements, I'd prefer we discuss things in private."

Three months ago, Avery had loved her job. Harper's predecessor had valued her opinion and trusted her instincts. He'd allowed her to do her job. All that had evaporated once Harper assumed control of the board and insisted she be consulted on every issue.

The more she delved into the business side of the shelter, the less Avery liked her job. Holding her hand out for donations and managing a staff weren't why she had gone to vet school. While she'd taken a couple of business classes in college in preparation for opening her own office, she hadn't enjoyed them.

When she'd accepted the shelter's offer, the board had hoped to hire an executive director within six months. She'd figured she could hold on until then, but that was over a year ago. The plan was that this year's Pet Walk would allow them to hire a director. Then she could focus on what she loved, taking care of animals and educating owners. So much for that.

"I know it's been hard for you to understand that working for a nonprofit organization in a small community means everyone knows your professional business, but that's a fact you need to adjust to," Harper said, her tone bordering on condescending.

Avery concentrated on her breathing, counted to ten and mentally listed Harper's good qualities. She truly cared about animals. Her heart was in the right place. She possessed valuable business connections and used them to recruit new shelter supporters. A great ambassador and advocate, she donated generously.

Her temper reined in, Avery said, "Our disagreements need to remain between us. You wouldn't want me to discuss problems I had with your shop or your merchandise in front of customers. I expect the same professionalism from you."

Realization dawned in Harper's eyes. "My mistake. I was upset about the news that we don't own the land. However, I do believe Reed could be a valuable resource for us."

The last person Avery wanted invading her professional life was Reed. "While he knows the corporate world, he lacks experience in the nonprofit arena and with fund-raising, and that's our biggest concern right now," Avery said in hopes of channeling the conversation to the task at hand. "The first thing we need to do is move up the date of the Pet Walk. I spoke with the executors. If we take out a loan to buy the land, the papers must be signed by the deadline. Since the land price is three hundred thousand, that means we need sixty thousand dollars for the down payment."

Harper paled. "The most we've ever raised from the Pet Walk is thirty-five thousand, and that was in a better economic climate."

Avery refused to let the shock and worry in Harper's voice rattle her further. They could do this. They had to. "Getting more and bigger sponsors is the key. I hope to tap some of my brothers' contacts."

Avery's oldest brother, Rory, modeled designer jeans for a large New York–based clothing company. Her brother Griffin was the host of the reality show *The Next Rodeo Star.* "If I can get Devlin Designs and Griffin's network to write us big checks, that'll go a long way to achieving our goal. However, the first thing we need to do is make sure that buying this land is our best option."

Harper tapped her manicured nail against the chair arm, something she did frequently as she thought. The habit grated on Avery's tightly strung nerves. "No matter what we do, we'll have to obtain a loan. To give us one, the bank will require proof we can afford the increase in our monthly operating costs."

Yesterday, Harper's micromanaging had been Avery's biggest problem. Now her shelter needed sixty thousand dollars to remain open, and the only man she'd ever loved was back. What she wouldn't give for a time machine.

FRIDAY AFTERNOON, REED sat jotting down discussion points for Monday's staff-status meeting as he waited for Jess in the school's pickup lane. Thank goodness for wireless technology to make productive use of otherwise wasted time.

The truck door flew open, Jess's backpack flew behind the seat and then the door slammed shut. He rolled down the passenger window. "Where are you going?"

"Out with friends."

"Get in. I'll drop you off after we talk."

"They're waiting for me."

"If I don't get more details, you don't go." Reed almost winced as similar things his father had said rang in his ears. He inhaled deeply before he continued. "Text them that I'll drop you off in a few minutes."

The door flew open again, and this time Jess crawled in, mumbling something about the Spanish Inquisition and teenagers having rights, too.

As the line of cars inched forward and Jess texted away, he asked about the specifics of her plans.

"We're going to hang out. We might go to a movie."

"What movie? Who with? What time will it be over?"

"I don't even know if we're going to a movie, so how can I know when it'll be over? Dad doesn't give me the third degree."

Reed wasn't sure if he believed her, but whether he did or not didn't matter. He was here, and Colt was in Afghanistan. Instead of saying that, he reiterated his stance that without enough details, she didn't go.

"We talked about going to the new Robert Pattinson movie, and before you ask, it's PG. I'll be home around eleven."

"Your dad said your curfew was ten-thirty."

"Whatever."

She was testing him and, he suspected, trying his patience on purpose. Did she really think her dad wouldn't tell him about her curfew or that he wouldn't remember? "How are you getting to the movie?"

"Jeez, my teachers ask less questions on quizzes. We were going to walk downtown and shop first, then go to McCabe's for pizza. If we go to a movie we'll walk. Otherwise we'll go back to Lindsey's house."

As he pulled out of the school parking lot onto the street, Reed said, "Text me when you know whether you're going to a movie or to a friend's house. I need to know where you are so I can pick you up."

Jess rolled her eyes. "You want to fit me with a GPS?"

"Don't tempt me," Reed said.

LATER THAT NIGHT, as Reed sat on the couch, a beer in his hand, watching the Colorado Rockies game, he thought over his first week. So far there hadn't been any major fires to put out at work. Most of his clients understood his situation. The two customers he'd been scheduled to visit next week had agreed to conference calls instead.

He and Jess had settled into a routine. To deal with the departure-time issue, he'd set all the clocks ahead five minutes, which meant they left for school relatively on time. After two days of him banging on her door at seven, Jess started getting up on her own. A success in his book, especially considering neither of them had done bodily harm to the other.

He stared at the spreadsheet in front of him, but couldn't focus. How pathetic was it to be working on Friday night? Usually he met friends for a couple of drinks. They talked shop, investments and sports. Or he'd go out on a date, although he hadn't done that in a while. After all, what were his chances of having a decent relationship with a woman with his parents' marriage as an example? Colt had tried that, only to end up with a less than pleasant foray into wedded bliss, and Colt wasn't nearly as like their father as Reed was.

He had to get out of the house before he went crazy. Not knowing what else to do, he snatched his cell phone off the coffee table and dialed Avery's number before he could reconsider. "Do you want to go out for pizza? You know, test out this friendship thing."

"I've got plans."

He told himself not to ask, because he wasn't jealous. He didn't want to know if she was seeing someone, but the words refused to stay put. "Hot date, huh?"

"Yup. It's Griffin and his wife Maggie's first night out since they had their baby, my gorgeous, amazing niece, Michaela. I'm meeting them at Halligan's."

"Griffin's a father? The world's ending, and I didn't have a clue." Her brother getting married and becoming a family man was like saying the Pope had become an atheist.

"He went on the reality show *Finding Mrs. Right*."

"So he married a gorgeous bachelorette?" Now, that made sense and sounded more like Avery's playboy brother.

"No, he didn't. How he and Maggie got together is actually a funny story."

"Tell me about it at Halligan's," Reed said, fishing for a formal invitation.

"You remember what the place is like, right? A down-home country bar. Not like the fancy California clubs you're used to where everyone's dressed to the nines and sits around sipping expensive wine and chatting about their investments."

Was that what she thought of him? How close she came to the truth shouldn't have stung, but it did. "Are you saying I won't fit in?"

"Between the peanut shells on the floor and the spilled beer, your expensive designer duds wouldn't last the night."

He couldn't miss her derisive tone, or the implication. He was a city boy now, wouldn't fit in and he no longer interested her. Now he was going no matter what she said. He had something to prove.

"I'll see you there."

"I'll be with my family."

"I've spent almost as much time with them as my own." And, with the exception of Colt, he had liked hers a whole hell of a lot better. "Are you saying you don't want me to come?"

"I know I said we could be friends, but I'm not sure I'm ready for us at Halligan's."

He knew what she meant. Us *together* at Halligan's. The down-home bar and grill had been everyone's favorite hangout, no matter their age. He and Avery had spent a lot of time together there. Laughing. Talking. Planning.

"It's Friday night. It's been a long week with Jess. Taking care of her and running my business long-distance is tougher than I expected." And the responsibility was weighing him down. "I need to get out, and I haven't spoken to anyone from town other than you since I left. Remember old man Aldridge and how pitiful he looked every Friday night?"

Tom Aldridge sat at the bar alone until he'd had a couple of beers. Then he wandered from table to table, telling the same lame jokes until someone finally took pity on him and asked him to join them.

"That could be me."

Silence met his request.

"What is it, Avery? You afraid you can't keep your hands off me?"

Avery's husky laugh reached deep inside him. "That'll be the day."

Chapter Four

As Avery sat at a table at the edge of the dance floor with Emma and her sisters-in-law, Elizabeth and Maggie, she still couldn't believe Reed had asked her out. Sort of. She'd almost dropped the phone. Though he'd added that they should test out "this friendship thing," warning bells had clanged so loudly in her head that her ears rang.

Part of her wanted to see what their relationship would be like now that they weren't fumbling teenagers. They'd always had great chemistry, and it had been so long since she'd wanted to be with a man.

The problem was she knew they couldn't have anything permanent, and she wasn't sure she could handle a casual relationship. She'd never done well with those.

"I talked with Mick," Emma said, referring to Halligan's owner. "He said we could put pitchers on the bar for donations. I thought I'd call you up onstage to explain what's going on with the shelter before we start our set."

"Sounds good." As Avery glanced again at the front door, she trailed her index finger through the condensation that had formed on her beer bottle. Luckily she faced the entrance, allowing her to keep her door preoccupation under wraps.

"What is it with you tonight?" Emma asked as she leaned closer.

"I keep thinking about work." She hoped her friend would be satisfied with her answer.

She was distracted all right, but not by her job. When she'd said they could start over as friends, she'd never expected Reed would press the issue. She'd imagined their truce would mean if they met on the street they'd smile, nod at each other and go on their way.

But once again she and Reed had different plans. Okay, so he wanted to test their new friendship. What was the big deal? As she'd told him, he wasn't irresistible.

Yummy and tempting, yes. Irresistible, no.

She possessed a decent amount of willpower, and a place with loud music and lots of people provided a great opportunity to test their new relationship. She could handle this.

If that were true, how come her stomach fluttered with butterflies as if she was waiting for her date to arrive?

"Liar." Emma's voice echoed the tiny one inside Avery's head. "Who are you watching for?"

So much for not appearing obvious. "Reed called and said he'd drop by tonight."

"Who's Reed?" asked Maggie, Griffin's wife.

"A high-school boyfriend." Avery tossed out an abbreviated, sanitized version of their past.

Questions flew at her.

"What's he like?" This from Elizabeth.

"How do you feel about him being back in town?" Maggie asked.

"Are you thinking about getting back together?" Again from Elizabeth.

"She said she's not interested," Emma scoffed.

"I can speak for myself, thank you." *Note to self. Never go out with friends when you're the only one not in a relationship. They feel compelled to meddle.* "Reed's different now than when we dated. He's gone all California-yuppie, arrogant CEO."

And they still wanted different things out of life.

"That's what I said about Griffin—that we had nothing in common and he was arrogant." Maggie's green eyes twinkled with amusement.

When Avery's brother had been the bachelor on *Finding Mrs. Right,* Avery had laughed herself silly watching her playboy brother date gorgeous women supposedly to find a wife. Instead of marrying one of the bachelorettes, he'd fallen for the average girl, the show's director, Maggie.

"Just because you could knock some sense into a man as thick-headed as my brother and make things work despite your differences doesn't mean everyone can."

"It's funny you said that, Maggie. I thought the same thing about Rory when we met, especially the arrogant part," said Elizabeth, Avery's other sister-in-law. "I think there's something to the saying opposites attract. Maybe you shouldn't write Reed off so fast, Avery."

Rory had met his wife on a horseback-riding tour on the family ranch. Elizabeth, a New York advertising executive, had offered Rory a modeling job, which he'd eventually accepted to earn the money to pay for their mother's first round of cancer treatments.

"You said Reed called you? Maybe he wants more than friendship," Maggie added.

"I heard he stood up for Avery when Harper got on her case. That doesn't sound like a man with nothing more than friendship on his mind to me," Emma said.

Avery glared at her friend, trying to send her a support-me-don't-pile-on look. "Don't you have to warm up your voice for your set, or test the speakers or something?"

Emma glanced at her watch. "I've got plenty of time."

"You don't think his calling means he wants to pick back up with you?" Elizabeth asked.

"What is it? National Find-Avery-A-Date Day and no one told me? Reed called because he was bored." Or at least that's what Avery told herself. He hadn't meant anything more.

"You said he grew up here. Why didn't he call an old *male* friend?"

Leave it to Maggie to pick up on that detail and have the nerve to ask the question.

"He said he hasn't kept in touch with anyone since he left." Avery thought about that. Granted, working on the ranch and studying to get top grades had left little time for friends, but he hadn't kept in contact with anyone? He really had left town and never looked back.

"But he kept in touch with you?" Maggie asked.

Avery shook her head and explained the reason for Reed's return. Then she told everyone how she'd run into him when she was at the Rocking M checking on a horse, and how she'd seen him again when he brought Jess's dog into the clinic.

"Wow. A single guy, suddenly having to parent a teenage girl, run his business long-distance and all without any friends or family for support. He's got a tough job ahead of him."

Avery knew that, but hearing Elizabeth say the words put things into a different perspective. She'd been so thrown off balance from seeing Reed that she hadn't thought of things from his point of view. He had taken on a huge undertaking and had no one he could count on.

He has you.

No. She refused to listen to the nagging voice that wanted her to save the world. She owed him nothing. Certainly not help. Not after all these years.

"If he doesn't want to get back together, why would he call you?" Emma tossed out.

"Quit making a big deal out of this. It's simple. He said I'm the only one he's talked to since he got back to town, and when he got bored he called me."

"Considering you two used to date, I'm surprised your mom hasn't taken Reed under her wing. She has a tendency to do that," Maggie said. "Not that I'm complaining."

Both Avery's sisters-in-law had firsthand experience with their mother-in-law's matchmaking. When Elizabeth first arrived in Estes Park to shoot a commercial, Avery's mom had insisted she stay at the ranch. When she'd balked, Nannette McAlister had said if Elizabeth didn't stay, there wouldn't be a commercial. That ended the discussion. Maggie had experienced similar subtle coercion when she and Griffin arrived to film the final episodes of *Finding Mrs. Right*.

"Don't give Mom any ideas. That's all I need—her going into matchmaker mode." Especially since her mother had always liked Reed, but only because Avery hadn't told her everything. Avery couldn't bring herself to tell anyone all that had happened. How she'd left messages on Reed's voice mail begging him to talk to her, and how she'd almost given up her desire to have children to keep him.

"That might not be all bad," Maggie countered, pulling Avery back to the conversation at the table.

"She did a pretty good job where Rory and I were concerned."

But her brothers had been different. Deep down inside, they both wanted the same things as their wives—a home and family. Unlike her and Reed. "I can handle my own love life, thank you very much."

Emma burst out laughing. "Not from what I can see. When was the last time you had a date?"

Longer than she wanted to admit or discuss. "That's not important."

Maggie stared at Avery, a curious look on her face. "Why don't you date more?"

Because she'd given up. Too many first dates that left her not wanting a second. She wanted someone who would still make her heart skip a beat when they really knew each other. A man she loved enough to overlook his annoying habits, and every man had a few of those.

When the trio at her table looked as if they'd launch into another inquisition, Avery raised her hand. "Leave it alone, okay? So I haven't been dating a lot. That doesn't mean going out with an old flame is a good idea."

"Doesn't mean it's a bad one, either," Emma said.

Choosing to ignore her friend's comment, Avery glanced at the entrance again to see the door open, and Reed step inside. The rosy glow of sunset framed him as he stood in the doorway dressed in formfitting jeans and a red-and-black-plaid shirt. Then she noticed his feet. Cowboy boots. Gone was the yuppie businessman.

Her pulse skyrocketed. He looked so relaxed, so approachable. As though he belonged here. He looked like the man she'd fallen in love with.

Not good.

She swallowed hard. A hand waved in front of her face. She turned to see Elizabeth grinning at her. "I'm guessing from the look on your face that's Reed?"

Avery nodded.

Maggie, the only one with her back to the door, actually scooted her chair around to get a better view. "He doesn't look very yuppie to me."

No, he didn't. Unfortunately.

Avery knew the minute he spotted her. He nodded, smiled and made his way toward her.

For a brief moment she wondered how big a scene it would cause and how much teasing she'd have to endure if she made a break for it and hid in the bathroom.

"Oh, he's delicious, and you want to just be friends? You either need your eyes checked or your standards are too high," Maggie teased.

No, what he wanted me to give up is too high a price to pay.

"He zeroed in on you the minute he walked in the door," Emma commented.

"And that's not a friendship look," Elizabeth added.

"It doesn't matter what he's thinking. That's all there's going to be between us," Avery responded as she stood. When a chorus of "Where are you going?" chimed out, she said, "If you think I'm letting Reed get anywhere near the three of you, you're crazy."

WHAT A TIME WARP, Reed thought as he stood inside the bar. Halligan's hadn't changed in the years he'd been gone. Formica-topped tables and industrial-style chairs littered the space. Wood paneling gave the place a warm, homey feel. The intoxicating smell of burgers wafted through the air.

Unlike being at the ranch and the house he'd grown up in, being in Halligan's didn't stir up bad memories. Instead the bar and grill conjured up images of him and Avery spending their nights playing pool and darts after they'd grabbed a burger. Here he'd been able to forget, at least for a while, the hell at home.

He spotted Avery seated at a table near the stage. Most women spent so much time, energy and money on their appearance, but not Avery. Her look was effortless, and always had been. Approachable. No matter what she wore, she possessed a grace, a natural beauty that very few women could compete with. His gaze locked on her as he started weaving his way through the maze of tables.

Would people see him as the successful businessman he'd worked to become or would they still view him as one of the poor Montgomery boys? No mother to care for them and a father who worked them every minute they weren't in school or sleeping. They'd pitied him without even knowing how bad things had been. Not even Avery or her family had known until the night he'd shown up at their door, the proof of his father's abuse discoloring his face. Until then his father had been smart enough to hit his sons where it wouldn't show for fear of losing his free ranch hands.

"Reed Montgomery? Damn, that can't be you?"

"Afraid so." He turned to see a blast from his past, slightly stockier than he remembered, but there was no mistaking that round face and lopsided grin. Brian Haddock, a friend from high school, strolled toward him, his hand outstretched.

"I was sorry to hear that Colt got deployed, but good thing he has you to come see to the ranch for him. That is, if you can remember which end of a horse to feed."

He shook his old friend's hand. "I think I remember. It's the end with fewer flies, right?"

Brian chuckled. "I never got the chance to thank you for all the help you gave me in physics our senior year. If it hadn't been for you, I'd have lost my football scholarship."

"I heard about your injury. Tough break."

After an amazing college football career as an offensive lineman at Colorado and being named an all-American, Brian had been drafted by the Chicago Bears in a late-round pick. Then in his first regular-season game, a freak accident on a broken play had ended his promising career.

"Luckily I had an education to fall back on. I have my own insurance company. What are you up to these days?"

"I own my own company, too. RJ Instruments. We manufacture computer chips for electronics."

Brian reached into his pocket, pulled out a business card and handed it to Reed. "I'm on the city government board of trustees. Your company's exactly the type we're trying to get to relocate here. Our new slogan is Move to the Mountains. We've got some great incentives."

With the cost of doing business in California rising he'd been mulling over relocating, but Estes Park? Not likely. Too many ghosts drifted around here, and not only at The Stanley Hotel.

"It's Friday night. I don't want to talk business. Call me next week, and we'll set up a time to talk." By then he'd have a polite no-thank-you response formulated.

"I'll do that. We can have lunch, my treat. We'll talk a little business and reminisce."

Reed's gaze locked on Avery, who'd either gotten

tired of waiting for him or had realized he needed rescuing, because she'd started walking toward him. "Excuse me, Brian, but I told Avery I'd meet her here, and I've left her waiting too long."

Avery, unaware of the enthralled males she left in her wake, stood out like a thoroughbred among mules. He shook his head. Where had that analogy come from?

Maybe it was true. You could take the boy out of the barn, but you couldn't wash all the manure off his boots.

He met her halfway to her table. "You were right. Halligan's hasn't changed a bit."

"I think the town would riot if anyone tried."

Once seated, Avery introduced Rory's wife, Elizabeth. He'd have put his money on the pretty, petite blonde being married to Griffin. Then Avery introduced him to her other sister-in-law, Maggie. Griffin's wife was the opposite of what he'd expected. She was tall, with shoulder-length dark hair. If it hadn't been for her striking green eyes, he'd have labeled her downright plain.

"So you're the woman who married Griffin."

Maggie shook her head. "I keep hearing how no one expected Griffin to marry. From the way everyone says that, you'd think I was one of the seven natural wonders."

"Even though I was a freshman and Griffin was a senior, I heard some pretty wild stories about him."

When Maggie smiled, the twinkle in her eyes told him she more than likely sent her husband on a merry chase. "We'll definitely have to talk. A woman never knows when she might need a secret weapon."

"Or blackmail material," Avery added.

The jovial banter reminded Reed of dinners in the

McAlister home. How many days had he sought refuge there when he couldn't face life in his own house?

"Reed Montgomery? You cost me five dollars. When my husband told me you'd come back to stay with Jess, I told him he'd lost his mind and bet him that he was wrong."

He stared at the slender waitress. Her face held more lines and her hair was now dusted with silver, but he recognized the face. "Hello, Mrs. Hughes. I'm sorry you lost the bet."

"That's all right, I'll win the next one, and call me Cathy." Genuine affection laced the woman's voice. "How are you and Jess getting along?"

The good news is we haven't knocked each other senseless yet. The bad news is that's still a possibility. "We had a rocky start, but things are getting better."

Mainly because they couldn't get any worse.

"I worry about her. Being a teenage girl is tough enough, but to have to go through those years without a mother around? No girl should have to deal with that."

Which was exactly why she should live with her grandparents. At least Colt's mother-in-law had raised a child. Of course, look how that had turned out, but weren't people supposed to learn from their mistakes? Even if they hadn't, certainly they'd do a better job than he would.

"It's good to see you. Now that your father's dead and buried, don't be such a stranger. I don't like to speak ill of the dead, but I'll make an exception with that man. When I heard what he'd been doing to you two boys all those years, well, being a good Christian woman I couldn't run him out of town on a rail, but I sure thought about it." She placed a delicate hand on his arm and leaned forward. "All the time you were in here, and I never knew what you were going through. If I had, I'd have hauled you out of that house myself, and made sure that man never got near you again. Anyone around here would have if we'd known."

The ache in his heart burned. He'd never suspected that. He'd felt so alone, when he needn't have.

"Now, what'll you have to eat? I see Mick giving me the evil eye from the bar because I'm standing here chatting too long." She nodded toward Halligan's owner. "I'm taking his order right now, so don't get your shorts in a knot." Then she returned her attention to Reed. "Our buffalo burgers are still the best you can find anywhere."

After Cathy took his order and left, Reed sat frozen in his seat, not sure what to say or do. His ghosts had definitely come out, but in a much different way than he'd expected.

"You okay?" Avery leaned toward him. "I'm sorry Cathy mentioned your dad. I know you never liked talking about him."

His phone sounded, alerting him to a text and saving him from having to deal with Avery's comment. He pulled his phone out of his pocket and scanned the text from Jess.

"More business?" Avery said, her tone filled with disapproval.

He shook his head. "It's from Jess. She's at the movies with friends. She was just letting me know what time I need to pick her up at the theatre."

Elizabeth said, "It's got to be hard suddenly being responsible for a teenager while running a company long-distance."

"Things got easier by the end of the week when I didn't have to use dynamite to blast Jess out of bed." She still retreated to her room after school, though, while he worked in her father's office. Then at dinner—that was rough. He'd had better conversations with former girlfriends than he did with Jess. "Teenage girls are an entirely different species. No matter what I say or do, she gets her nose out of joint."

"One time my brothers got so upset with my moods—" Maggie flashed air quotes "—they threatened to lock me in a closet."

"Now, that's a thought."

"I didn't have any problems with her when you two picked up Thor," Avery said. "We got along well."

"You speak the same female language." His niece and Avery's comfortable interaction made his inability to connect with Jess that much more obvious, reinforcing the fact that he wasn't meant to have a family.

The ping of guitars tuning up floated through the room.

"I can't believe it. Our husbands are walking this way," Elizabeth said, pointing toward the poolroom.

"I thought we'd have to hunt them down to dance," Maggie added.

Reed stiffened as Avery's brothers approached. What did they know about what had happened between him and Avery? He searched the men's faces. No sign of anger. They hadn't charged him yet, screaming that they planned to tear him apart. Maybe, since Rory had been in college and Griffin on the rodeo circuit when he and Avery broke up, they didn't know all the gory details.

"Reed here tells me he has some pretty interesting stories about you," Maggie said when her husband stood beside her.

Griffin kissed his wife on the cheek. "That was all before I met you. I'm older and wiser now."

Maggie laughed. "At least half the time."

"I'd say more like twenty-five percent," Rory quipped before he turned to Reed. "If you have any problems around the ranch, let me know. I'll be glad to help out."

The unexpected offer caught Reed off guard. "Thanks, I'll keep that in mind."

Griffin turned to Reed. "Man, Colt threw you into the deep end of the pool, didn't he? I don't know if I could take suddenly being responsible for a teenager. Talk about scary."

"Watch what you say," Rory's wife teased. "Half the people at this table used to be teenage girls."

Rory put his arm around his wife. "You're wonderful now, and I'd be lost without you, but you've got to admit teenage girls can be frightening."

"Like you guys have room to talk," Avery said. "You two were idiots when you were teenagers."

Reed glanced at the smiling faces surrounding him as the good-natured gibes bounced around the table. Cracks had flown around his family's table, but not like these ones. His dad's had been meant to pierce the skin. Everyone left the table bruised one way or another.

"I didn't understand girls when I was in high school. Throw in all the changes in society since I graduated, and I don't know what to do most of the time," Reed said.

"No one does," Rory added.

"My plan is to lock Michaela in her room when she turns thirteen and let her out when she's thirty." A look of horror passed over Griffin's face. "And I don't even want to think about dating."

Maggie patted her husband's hand and smiled. "I can't believe you're worried about that already. She's only six weeks old."

Avery laughed. "Watching you raise a daughter is going to be so much fun."

Reed shuddered. "Thank God Jess isn't dating or talking about boys." That would send him over the edge into complete insanity.

"I bet she's talking about boys, just not to you," Avery added.

"Don't tell me that." Reed clutched his heart, only half in jest. Dealing with boy troubles could give him a heart attack. "You're not helping my stress level."

From up on stage, a female spoke into the microphone, commanding their attention.

"I'm glad we've got a good crowd tonight, because the Estes Park animal shelter needs your help." The speaker turned to their table. "Avery, come up and give everyone the details."

"Excuse me—duty calls," Avery said as she stood. Once on the stage, she continued, "We've found out we don't own the land our building sits on. To keep the shelter open and to obtain a loan, we've got to raise the money for a down payment. We've got pitchers on the bar. Ours are the ones with the dog collars wrapped around them. When you pick up a drink and tip the bartenders, think about all the good work the shelter does, and drop a few bucks in our pitcher, too. Now, let's have some fun!"

As the band started playing, memories of him and Avery listening to country-and-western music and dancing on this same floor stirred within him. How often had he lost himself in her arms? She'd been his refuge.

After her brothers and their wives left to dance, he sat waiting for Avery. They had such a history, but when he tried to talk to her tonight he was about as smooth as a gravel road. You'd think this was a first date. He thought about what she'd said on the stage. The shelter needed money because they didn't own the land their building sat on. Land wasn't cheap. Raising that kind of cash could be tough in this economy. When she returned, he asked, "How much money do you need to raise for the down payment?"

"Sixty thousand."

"Putting a pitcher on a bar and asking for donations won't get you that kind of money."

"I know. That's why I'm moving up the date for our annual Pet Walk."

"What's a Pet Walk? Can it raise the kind of money you need?"

"People pay a registration fee to come with their pet. We have vendors selling things, food and contests. It's like a carnival for people and pets. We have some attendees who raise money by getting pledges for walking at the event. One year we raised thirty-five thousand."

"That's a long way from getting the down payment."

"Earlier you said you didn't want to talk about work. I don't, either." She stood. "Let's dance."

He watched the other couples. Some of the moves looked the same. "I haven't line danced in years."

"Suit yourself." She tossed the words over her shoulder with a sly grin as she headed for the dance floor, leaving him sitting by himself.

She glanced his way, hooked her thumbs in her jeans pockets and glided to the left swaying her hips. She licked her lips and smiled, a tempting, see-what-you're-missing kind of grin. Her step held an extra bounce. Her skin glowed from exertion. He resisted the urge to wipe his moist palms on his jeans and sat glued to his seat, mesmerized. On the outside looking in.

The sexy minx is taunting me.

The woman probably enjoyed poking sleeping bears, too. Damned if he'd let her challenge go unanswered. He held her gaze as he stood and walked toward her. When he reached her, she stared him down. "Finally screwed up your courage, huh?"

"The moves look pretty much the same. I bet line dancing's like riding a bicycle."

It took only a minute for him to realize how wrong he'd been. He invariably went left when he should have gone right. He stomped his foot when he should've tapped his heel and kicked. Making a fool of himself wasn't how he had envisioned the night going.

Halfway through the first dance he huffed and puffed to keep up, something that shouldn't be happening considering how much he worked out. Then he sidestepped when he should've kicked, and came close to running into her. Focusing on his footwork, he prayed he wouldn't stomp on her foot. The thought no sooner zipped through his head then he did exactly that. "Sorry."

Way to impress a beautiful woman. Almost knock her down and then tromp on her foot.

"Luckily I'm wearing boots. Otherwise you'd be in trouble." She sashayed beside him, making him remember how graceful she'd always been. Then he whirled around and bumped into a short fortysomething man who looked vaguely familiar. The slight man swayed on his feet. Reed reached out to steady him and ended up wrapping his arms around him instead. He righted the gentleman and stepped away, embarrassment racing through his veins. "You okay?"

Could this get any worse?

"I'm fine, Reed, son. Good to see you back, and don't

you worry. I'd be a mite distracted, too, if I was danc-ing with a pretty thing like Avery."

"Now we're going to slow things down," said the singer/guitarist who'd called Avery up on stage earlier. "We've had a request from Griffin McAlister for the first song he and his wife, Maggie, danced to here at Halligan's."

Reed smiled. Finally he'd be able to put his arms around Avery the way he'd wanted to all night.

"I don't know about you, but I think it's time for a cold beer." Her chest rose and fell rapidly.

No way was she getting away from him. Not after he'd endured her teasing about his moves. He slipped his arm around her waist as he pulled her closer. "Are you still afraid you can't keep your hands off me?"

Her chin tilted up. Apparently she still couldn't turn down a challenge. He almost grinned, but controlled the urge for fear of scaring her off.

She slipped her right hand into his, while her left slid up his chest. His pulse accelerated. The simple touch was surprisingly electric. Maybe this hadn't been a good idea.

What was wrong with them sharing each other's company? They were both adults. He should just enjoy this, and if it led to more, they could handle it.

"Nice dip with Mr. Hendricks, by the way," Avery teased, her eyes twinkling with amusement. "You used to be a great dancer."

"Maybe you should give me private lessons."

"Check line dancing on Google and watch a video."

He should stick to them being friends and lay off the innuendos, but he couldn't help himself. Now that he held Avery in his arms, the idea of leaving things at friendship felt unsatisfying.

As they swayed to the music, the lyrics about a cowboy on the road missing his girl floated over him. Avery's familiar earthy scent swirled around him. He remembered how he'd lost himself in her when things got rough at home. She'd been the anchor he clung to, the quiet in his life amid the storm of his father's tirades and abuse. He'd often wondered how different life would've been if he'd grown up in a household like the McAlisters'.

He leaned closer until his lips rested beside her ear. How long had it been since he'd allowed himself to get close to someone?

"Do you wonder what it would be like between us now?" he asked.

He sure as hell did. Ever since she'd walked out of the stall in Colt's barn. The images had kept him awake and throbbing more than one night since he'd returned.

"No." Her expressive eyes and her breathy voice contradicted her statement.

"Right now I'm wondering." His lips pressed against the tender skin behind her ear, and he felt her shiver. Her head rested on his shoulder, and her warmth seeped into him. Need overrode what little common sense he possessed. Hell, common sense was overrated, anyway.

His lips traced a path down her neck, while his hand caressed her lower back, encouraging her to get even closer. Her thighs brushed his groin, and she gasped. Her gaze locked with his, and he couldn't resist her. He lowered his mouth to hers and gently covered her lips, searching and testing. To hell with everything but her and him together.

She nuzzled the sensitive spot behind his ear. Being with her like this felt right.

His phone vibrated in his pocket. His heart hammered so loudly he wondered if she could hear the beat over the band. Dazed and strung tighter than a barbed-wire fence, he stepped away, instantly feeling cut adrift. He dug his phone out of his pocket and glanced at the screen. Estes Park Police Department.

"Avery, I have to take this."

She folded her arms across her chest, anger replacing passion in her gaze. "Are you so worried about staying connected, about your business, that you can't miss a call?" She shook her head. "You're going to miss out on what's really important in life, Reed."

Chapter Five

His pulse rate still revving, Reed watched Avery storm off and then worked his way through the couples on the dance floor, heading for the front door.

"Reed Montgomery? This is Officer Blume."

"Is it Jess? Is she okay?"

"She's fine, but I've got her here at the station. I understand you're her guardian while her father's gone."

As his heart rate slowed and his panic subsided, his anger kicked in. Jess had texted him earlier to say she was going to a movie with friends. He glanced at his watch. He was to pick her up at the theater in half an hour. She'd lied to him. "What happened?"

"She spray-painted graffiti on the animal shelter."

He told the officer he was coming and climbed into his truck. Colt hadn't mentioned things about Jess doing anything that would get her in trouble with the law.

Wait a minute. Jess vandalized the shelter? That didn't make sense. She and Avery had gotten along well when they'd picked up Thor. A lot of the irritation that filled Jess's voice when she talked to him had been absent with Avery. Something wasn't right. His gut told him Jess wouldn't damage the shelter. Someplace else, maybe, but not where Avery worked.

What the hell was he going to do about this, and how could he tell his brother that Jess had gotten hauled into the police station?

Deal with the police first. Then worry about telling Colt.

And he refused to think about Avery and how good it had felt to hold her. How kissing her had him remembering all their good times and made him wonder if leaving her had been the biggest mistake of his life.

As Avery left the dance floor, she tried to deny that Reed's touch had sent more excitement and electricity bolting through her than she'd felt in years. When he'd kissed her, she'd forgotten everything but him.

How had she let things get this out of control? And how did she set them right again? How dare he think he could stroll into town and pick up with her as if he'd never left?

Agreeing to dance with him. That's where things went wrong. Touching Reed. Big mistake. She'd set out to prove something to herself, and she sure had. She'd proved she had less willpower than she'd thought where he was concerned.

New survival game plan—stay as far from Reed as possible.

Her phone rang. The screen revealed the number of the Estes Park police. Her mom—had something happened? Please, no. She glanced around the bar and saw both her brothers. If something had happened, the authorities would call Rory first, but maybe he hadn't heard his phone. Panic making her heart race, she answered the call and stepped outside.

"Dr. McAlister, this is Officer Blume. I need you to

come to the police station. A group of teenagers vandalized the shelter."

Thank God, her mother was fine. Vandalism she could handle. Officer Blume proceeded to tell her that the teenagers had scattered when they arrived, but they'd managed to apprehend one suspect. She told the officer she'd be there in a few minutes, and rushed back into Halligan's to offer a quick explanation to her family.

As she headed for the police station she wondered why teenagers would vandalize the shelter. They'd never had any issues like this before. Were these simply bored kids or was this caused by someone's frustration with the shelter?

When Avery parked at the police station, Reed emerged from the truck beside her. "What are you doing here?" she asked.

"The police picked up Jess for vandalism. That's the call I got at the bar."

Avery joined him on the sidewalk, her head spinning. "Jess? When the police told me teenagers had vandalized the shelter, the last one I would've suspected was Jess. There has to be some mistake. She wouldn't do that. Not when she adopted Thor from us."

"That's exactly what I thought, but the police caught her there with a spray can. They also said she won't tell them anything, especially not who else was there."

"You mean *you* don't know who she was with?"

"She mentioned a friend named Lindsey, but not her last name." Reed pinched the bridge of his nose. "I asked her so many questions about what she was doing tonight. How could I forget to ask for full names of her friends?"

"This is all new to you, and there's a lot to remember."

He straightened. "You can bet I'll get the whole story out of her now."

The hard set of Reed's mouth and his clenched fists surprised her. She'd never been afraid of him in all the years she'd known him, but she'd seen glimpses of anger when he talked about his father.

And there had been that one night after graduation when he'd shown up at her door, purple and blue discoloring his swollen cheek. He'd collapsed against her and confessed how his father had been beating him for years. He'd told her how things had grown worse since Colt moved away. Without his brother there to defuse matters, Reed nearly beat his father to death.

Once he'd stopped shaking, she'd coaxed him into the chair in her father's study while she woke her parents. After quickly explaining the situation, she begged them to help Reed.

Her father called his lawyer and the two men shut themselves in her father's office with Reed. Then the police arrived. Afterward, Reed wouldn't tell her anything other than that, thanks to her father, he wouldn't go to jail. Her father likewise refused to supply details, claiming it wasn't his place.

"Don't assume the worst and jump on Jess the minute you see her. Give her a chance to explain," Avery said now.

"As long as she tells me exactly what happened we'll be fine."

"And if she won't? Remember, you're dealing with a fourteen-year-old. You promised Colt you'd be flexible."

"And I will be. I don't care who she talks to about what happened, but she *will* talk."

"Adding your current mindset to typical teenager attitude won't be productive or pretty." Avery clasped

Reed's arm, halting him. Tense muscles rippled under her palm. "What's going on here? I know Jess is in trouble, but she wasn't picked up for doing drugs or drinking. She hasn't hurt anyone. Why are you so angry?"

"Why aren't you more upset? She vandalized your shelter."

"Don't change the subject." She inched closer and squeezed his arm. "Tell me why you're so upset."

He jerked away, rejecting her comfort. Fine, that was probably best for both of them. She wouldn't make the mistake of offering it again.

"I'm responsible for Jess. She's been testing me. I've got to show her I won't tolerate this. No, it wasn't drugs or something worse. *This* time."

"I know you take your guardian role seriously. That's who you are." She wanted to hold him, ease his fears, and the thought left her shaken. "You're worried Jess's behavior tonight could lead to bigger issues, and it's your job to ensure that doesn't happen."

"Damn right it is."

"Jess has always been a good kid. I think there's something else going on here. Is she acting out because her dad's gone? Is she hanging around with the wrong crowd? Guys focus on getting the facts and finding a solution, but you're dealing with a teenage girl. You need to find out *why* she did this. You can't just get angry with her."

The shelter was her problem, not why Jess was acting out. Helping Reed and getting attached to him and his niece would complicate her life, but more important, it would take time and energy away from her job. And she could so easily get emotionally involved—but she couldn't forget what had driven them apart.

Still, she thought of Jess, and how Reed's current

mood could react with hers to make things worse. Avery stepped closer and reached out to him, but pulled back at the last moment. Instead, she peered up at him. "Reed, lighten up. She hasn't joined the Mafia. She spray-painted the shelter. This is very fixable."

His stance softened as he reached for her hand. He clasped her fingers so tightly she almost winced. "I'm glad you're here. You always helped me keep things in perspective. I'm so scared of messing up. What do I know about kids? Look at the example I had for a father."

Her heart ached for the pain his father had caused, both emotionally and physically. Staring into his worried gaze, she wished he hadn't said anything. How could she leave him alone to deal with the situation after what he'd just said?

"We'll handle this together."

"Thanks." He released her hand, took a deep breath and smiled faintly. "I'm going to hold you to that."

When they walked into the police station, Officer Blume met them at the front desk. "Someone driving by on the highway saw a group of teenagers spray-painting the shelter." The officer faced Reed. "Your niece was the only one caught at the scene. She won't tell us anything. We checked her phone and have an idea of who was with her, but unless she corroborates that, all the blame falls on her." Officer Blume turned to Avery. "Does the shelter want to press charges?"

"If it were up to me, I'd let things go with restitution, but it's shelter policy that we prosecute in cases like this," Avery said to both men.

"Would you give us a minute alone?" Reed asked the officer.

The other man nodded. "I'll finish the paperwork for your niece's release and be back in a minute."

Once he and Avery were alone, Reed said, "There isn't any way you can avoid pressing charges?"

"I'm afraid not. Since it's a shelter policy, there's nothing I can do. I'm sorry. If I could let things go at restitution, I really would."

He nodded. "Thanks for that. How am I going to tell Colt Jess got arrested?"

The weariness in his voice tugged at her heart. He really was in over his head. "Colt will understand. She's a teenager. They do stupid stuff like this." She placed her hand on his arm, and he placed his hand over hers. "Now you know more, and you'll watch her closer for other signs of problems."

"I don't know if I can do this. It's so much responsibility. That's why I never—"

Though he cut himself off, she knew what he'd been about to say.

That's why I never want to have kids.

She pulled away and walked across the waiting room to sit in one of the wooden chairs against the wall.

She wouldn't get involved with Reed again. Some risks were worth taking and some were just plain foolish because the odds of succeeding sucked. Having a relationship with Reed fell into the latter category. She'd help him with Jess, but that was as far as things would go. She hadn't been willing to compromise all those years ago and give up having children, and she couldn't now.

When Officer Blume returned with Jess's release papers, Avery reiterated that the shelter would be pressing charges. As the officer went to get Jess, Avery and Reed stood awkwardly beside each other.

"You lied to me," Reed said the minute the teenager arrived. His low voice rippled with restraint.

"No, I didn't. When I talked to you, I was at the movie, but it was lame, and we left."

"Then you should've called me to pick you up. What the hell were you thinking? You committed a crime."

Jess stood there, her body rigid, her arms crossed, looking at the floor.

Reed shoved his hands into his front pockets. "I want to know who you were with and why you did this."

"I don't want to talk about it."

Why couldn't Reed see his heavy-handed attitude was only making Jess more adamant to best him? Avery stepped forward and placed her hand on the teenager's arm, but Jess refused to meet her gaze. "Why would you do this to the shelter?"

"It wasn't me," Jess insisted.

"The police caught you there with spray-paint cans," Reed said.

"I was there, but I didn't do anything."

"Then who the hell did?" Reed fired back.

Jess fidgeted with the hem of her black skull-print T-shirt. "I tried to talk them out of it, but no one would listen. Really I did." Jess finally met Avery's gaze. Guilt shone in her eyes.

"I believe you, sweetheart." Avery wrapped her hands around the girl's icy ones. Her mind raced trying to recall who Jess's friends were and why they would damage the shelter, but nothing came to mind. But then, who could figure out how teenagers' brains worked, or rather, didn't work? "You've got to tell us who was with you."

"I can't."

Reed held out his hand, practically shoving it under

his niece's nose. "Give me your cell phone. I bet you've got texts that'll shed light on what happened."

Jess stepped back. "You're not my father. You've got no right to look at my phone because you don't pay for it, and there's nothing on it that implicates anyone."

"That's all right. I'll get the information another way." Reed's strong voice rang with unflinching authority. "The police checked your phone. I'll get Lindsey's last name from them. Then I'll call her parents."

Jess squeezed Avery's hands so tightly her knuckles cracked. "I'll say she wasn't there, and then there's nothing the police can do."

"A crime was committed and your friends need to be held accountable for their actions."

"I can't tell the police. You don't know what it's like in high school." Jess's panicked gaze locked on Avery. "Tell him he can't do this. I'm already a freak—the girl whose mom ran off with the computer-repair guy and got herself killed. There are people who don't want anything to do with me because of that. If I squeal on my friends, I'll be a complete outcast."

Avery tried to catch Reed's eye, but his stare remained focused on Jess. Things had always been black-and-white to him.

"Then that's the price you'll have to pay," Reed said.

"That's easy for you to say. You won't be the one sitting alone at lunch while all your former friends sit at another table whispering about you."

"What kind of friends are they if they ran off and left you to take the blame?" Avery asked, hoping to make Jess see how she'd misplaced her loyalty.

"I'll find out who Lindsey is, so you might as well tell me." Reed ground out the words.

"How can you do this to me?" Jess's voice broke and

her eyes filled with tears. She turned to Avery. "Can't you make him understand?"

Avery glanced between the stubborn pair. Neither one showed any signs of backing down. Someone had to play peacemaker. "Reed, can I talk to you in private?"

"There's nothing to talk about."

"Please?"

Avery's soft plea and the worried look in her eyes when she placed her hand on his arm pulled him back to reality. The anger stirring inside him startled him. Worse yet, it reminded him of his father.

A vision of the man, his eyes bulging, nostrils flaring as he railed at him, flashed in his mind. Was that how he looked to Jess and Avery?

He turned and walked across the room, his knees growing weak, Avery beside him.

"Being a hard-ass isn't working. All it's doing is making her more adamant about protecting her friends. You have to back down. Colt told me about Jess threatening to run away. She can only take so much."

"I know. I don't think she would really do it, but just because she's threatened to run away doesn't mean I can overlook what she's done or the fact that she won't tell the police who was with her. She has to tell them everything."

"Can't you see she's not going to? All you're doing is alienating her."

"She vandalized your shelter. You should be backing me up and helping me get the names out of her. Instead, you're coddling her and encouraging her to defy me." Reed shoved his hands into his pockets. "She's being overly dramatic about her friends' reaction."

"No, she's not. You don't know what girls can be like,

or how fragile their psyches are. She could be right that her friends would ostracize her."

"We're talking a legal issue here, Avery."

"I know, but I'm more concerned about her emotional state. If she's willing to take the fall for her friends, let her. My mom and dad used to talk about natural consequences. They said those were often worse than any punishment they could give us. Lay things out for her, that if she won't tell on her friends, the natural consequence is she'll end up in juvenile court to take all the blame. It might teach Jess a good lesson about friendship."

What Avery said made sense, though he balked at the idea of letting Jess's friends get away with a crime. But those kids weren't his problem. Jess was. "Maybe you're right, and I should let her face the consequences."

"Trust me."

The words hung heavy between them and had nothing to do with the situation surrounding Jess. "I always have."

Avery nibbled on her lower lip. "I think letting the court deal with Jess is the wisest thing to do."

He nodded, whatever might have passed between them now gone. When they rejoined Jess, he said, "I'll ask you one more time to tell me who was with you, and before you answer, be aware that the shelter's policy is always to press charges in cases like these. Dr. McAlister has no say in the matter. That means when the shelter presses charges you'll end up in juvenile court, and there won't be anyone else to take the blame."

"I understand," Jess said, though he doubted she truly grasped the implications of her decision. "I'd rather go to court than betray my friends."

"I admire your loyalty, Jess, but I think your uncle's

right," Avery added. "Your friends don't deserve you." Then she turned to him. "Will you two be okay if I head home? I have an early surgery scheduled for tomorrow."

Reed nodded, the anger he'd felt gone, thanks to Avery. What would he have done if she hadn't been here to help him, to smooth things over when he'd been on the brink of letting his frustration consume him?

He couldn't even think about what might have happened.

THE NEXT MORNING REED stared at his brother's image on the computer screen as he updated Colt on his daughter's antics. "I'm out of my league here. You've got to talk to Jess about what happened. Make her tell you who she was with."

"I'll talk to her, but my guess is she won't tell me any more than she told you. When Jess makes up her mind, there's no changing it."

Reed chuckled. "Sounds like someone else I know."

"Yeah, you." His brother laughed. "For what it's worth, I would've handled things the same way you did. As a parent, I've learned sometimes I have to let my kid fall flat on her face."

"Her friends shouldn't be getting away with this."

"They're not my problem. I'm more worried that Jess got pulled into this stunt. I thought she had more sense than to go along with the crowd."

"I'm screwing up with her. I can handle running my own company, but dealing with Jess is bringing me to my knees." His voice broke and he paused to collect himself. "I'm saying things that sound so damned much like our father."

"You're nothing like that bastard, if that's what you're worried about." His brother's confident reassurance offered Reed little comfort. "Have you had any luck with getting the association to make an exception for Jess?"

"Not so far, but my lawyer's working on it." He explained about the federal act. "Have you talked to your in-laws? Do they have an idea when they can come stay with Jess?"

"I got an email from them the other day. Joanne's doing better. She started physical therapy, but she's not up to traveling yet."

"What do you think about me threatening to go to the media if the association won't change its position?"

"I guess I don't have a problem with that, but I'm still not sure Jess is better off with them." Colt turned to the voices escalating in the background. "I gotta go. I'll talk to Jess as soon as I can and I'll back you up. Don't worry. You're doing better than you think."

"Stay safe."

After his brother responded with a quick "Will do," they were disconnected. Reed shook his head. He was doing better than he thought? In what universe?

He couldn't risk losing control with Jess, or making bigger mistakes. He picked up his phone, called his lawyer and asked what he'd found out.

"I checked on the occupancy issue, and they're in compliance."

With the way his luck had been running of late, why did that not surprise him? "Threaten to contact the local media, and if the association doesn't concede, do it."

"Are you sure that's what you want to do? There's an outside chance it could backfire and be bad publicity for the company."

"It won't backfire. We're talking about a widowed soldier and his teenage daughter. The public support will be overwhelming."

He was done being nice. Time to play hardball before he messed up even worse with Jess.

Two days later, Reed and Jess stood before Juvenile Court Judge Hoffman.

After Reed had taken away her cell phone and grounded her per Colt's instructions, Jess had adopted a two-pronged approach to dealing with him—avoiding him and pretending he was invisible. He figured the justice system would take care of punishing her further, but their strained relationship had started wearing on him.

"You're not doing a very good job as a guardian, Mr. Montgomery." The judge stared down at Reed from his seat behind the massive oak bench, the American and Colorado flags standing watch behind him.

No kidding. Thanks for letting me in on that secret.

"Taking care of a teenager is new to me, Your Honor." Weariness seeped into him. He felt as if he'd aged ten years since he'd met Jess at the airport. At this rate, he'd die of old age in three weeks.

"If you don't have the skills to do the job, then you'd better find a way to get them. You've been given a huge responsibility. Your brother's in Afghanistan serving our country. He shouldn't have to worry about his daughter. It's time to cowboy up."

When Judge Hoffman looked as if he expected a response, Reed replied, "Yes, sir."

"Young lady, I hear you refuse to tell the police who was with you Friday night," Judge Hoffman continued, his stern voice booming through the courtroom.

"I was alone." Jess crossed her arms over her chest. What could be seen of her coffee-colored eyes through the long bangs hanging in her face blazed with teenage defiance.

His teenage-girl-remote-island idea looked better all the time.

"The witness said she saw four teenagers," Judge Hoffman countered.

"I won't betray my friends."

"That concerns me. Protecting your friends when they commit crimes is not using good judgment." Judge Hoffman's gaze scanned the gallery. "What do you have to say about all this, Dr. McAlister?"

Avery, dressed in a black skirt and white blouse, stood and moved forward. Reed couldn't help staring. He remembered her having great legs, but not ones that belonged on a pin-up poster.

"While I can't overlook what Jess did, I understand her reluctance to be more forthcoming. Teenage girls can be very cruel, especially if they feel betrayed, and that's likely to be how her peers will see her talking to the authorities." Avery glanced toward Reed and Jess. "From what Jess told me, there has been unkind talk about her mother. She fears if she names names things will get worse."

The judge nodded. "I'm well aware of how insensitive teenagers can be. I also understand how difficult losing her mother must have been and now having her father in Afghanistan, but it can't excuse her behavior."

"I agree, but what Jess needs right now is guidance and stability," Avery responded. "My mom was such a big source of advice and support for me as a teenager. I can't imagine what I would've done without her at Jess's age."

"Thank you for your input, Dr. McAlister." Judge Hoffman shuffled through the papers in front of him. "I don't have a repair estimate. Do you have that information?"

She handed the bailiff a packet of paper. "Max at Jenson's Paint has given me an estimate. Now, the labor to have the building painted would be—"

"The labor's not going to cost anything because Miss Montgomery's going to paint over her artwork." Judge Hoffman jotted down something before his gaze returned to Jess. "You're at a crossroads, young lady. I'm hoping my actions will make you think about choosing a better path than the one you're on right now. I also suggest you take a good hard look at your friendships, and the fact that those you were with left you to take the blame. That says a lot about their character."

"Yes, sir," Jess replied.

"I want to make it clear that I won't tolerate further shenanigans," the judge continued. "Jessica Montgomery, I sentence you to thirty hours of community service to be served at the Estes Park animal shelter. That's in addition to however long it takes you to paint over your little art project." He turned his focus to Reed. "Mr. Montgomery, you need to keep a closer eye on your niece and work on your relationship."

Reed nodded. Wanting to work on his relationship with Jess wasn't the problem. How to do it was his stumbling block.

"Now, Dr. McAlister, I'm glad to hear you say you feel Miss Montgomery needs guidance, particularly from a wiser, older female. While I can't require it of you, I'd like to see you personally supervise her at the shelter. You're a respected member of our community, and Miss Montgomery would greatly benefit from interaction with you. I'd also like you to keep in touch with me as to her progress."

Avery's first reaction was to blurt out that with the shelter in such financial trouble she didn't have time to work with a teenager who had issues, but she couldn't. She couldn't risk offending Judge Hoffman, not when he was one of the people she'd hit up to write a nice fat check. Instead of giving in to her frustration, she plastered a smile on her face. "Your Honor, I'll be happy to work with Miss Montgomery at the shelter. Our next volunteer orientation is at the end of September. I'll get the information to her."

"I want her volunteering as soon as possible." The judge's narrow gaze locked on Jess. "You obviously have too much free time on your hands, young lady, and I intend to fill some of it immediately."

"I'll be happy to put Jess to work as soon as possible."

"See that you do, Dr. McAlister. I trust you and Mr. Montgomery to work out those details as well as the ones associated with getting the shelter painted." The judge banged his gavel, and the bailiff called for the next case.

If only she could dismiss this case as easily. What she wouldn't give for one of those little gizmos from *Men in Black* right now. She'd pop on her shades and zap Reed's memory about the other night at Halligan's clean so he'd forget how she'd practically crawled inside his skin when he kissed her. That would make dealing with him now much easier.

Unfortunately, she'd have to tough it out the old-fashioned way—by pretending the incident had never happened.

Chapter Six

When Reed and Jess joined her outside the court-room, Avery focused on the teenager rather than Reed. "There's something I need to know, and I expect an answer. I think I deserve one, since you adopted Thor from us." After Jess nodded, Avery continued, "Do you think your friends will do further damage to the shelter?"

"I don't think so. They were pretty freaked out and upset by me getting caught."

"Not enough that they owned up to what they did," Reed said.

"They did say they were sorry," Jess added.

Avery could see Reed preparing to launch into another pointless lecture. Before he could, she said, "As far as I'm concerned, we're starting over. As long as you do a good job at the shelter, we won't have any problems. Everyone deserves a second chance. But if you hear anyone talking about vandalizing the shelter again, please let me know so I can take precautions."

Jess nodded.

Avery turned her attention to Reed. He looked so handsome dressed in rancher chic, meaning he'd added a sport coat to his black jeans and T-shirt. Her heart fluttered, and she ignored her budding emotions. "We need to get something straight. Our policy is that volunteers Jess's age must be accompanied by an adult. The shelter isn't a drop-off center."

"I wasn't sentenced to community service."

Like she was any happier about this than he was? If she had her way, she'd avoid him like a friend with the flu. "It's our policy, and I can't make an exception. If you don't volunteer with Jess, she won't be able to fulfill her community service."

She could almost see past his steely blue gaze to the gears churning in his head as he searched for a loophole to wiggle through.

"Lucky you, to get two volunteers for the price of one."

Lucky wasn't the word she'd have chosen. "I'll expect you both at the shelter tomorrow after school with whatever Max says you need to paint the shelter."

Reed and Jess stood outside the shelter, paint supplies spread out at their feet. Reed stared at the words *Animals shouldn't be in jail* sprayed across the shelter wall in brightened paint. "What do you think of your friends now that you're here and they're out there having fun?"

Jess shrugged. "Since I'm grounded, the teachers don't let us talk in class, and my phone's locked up, so I haven't seen or talked to my friends much."

"I'm not sure that's a bad thing, since they hung you out to dry. They should be here helping you." He pulled a roll of blue painter's tape out of the bag of supplies they'd purchased and twirled the roll between his fingers. "What do you know about painting a building?"

"You mean there's more to it than dunking the roller in the paint and moving it over the wall?"

He explained how she needed to tape around the

windows and trim, then pointed to a place where the paint had flaked off. "You need to use the scraper we bought to make sure the surface is smooth before you paint. Otherwise it'll just peel again."

"How do you know so much about painting?"

He thought about the judge's comment that he work on his relationship with Jess. Now was as good a time as any. "What's your dad told you about when he was a kid?"

"Not much. One time I asked him how he learned to be such a good dad, and he told me that he just remembered what his father did and did the opposite."

"That sounds just like your dad." Colt could learn from the roughest experiences and come out better for having survived. "I learned how to paint a house when your dad was sixteen and I was your age. Our dad made us paint the house. I wanted to just jump in and get the job done. Your dad talked with the guy at the paint store to make sure we knew what we were doing."

"Didn't your dad show you what needed to be done?"

"He wasn't big on doing much work or explaining what needed to be done. He preferred criticizing afterward."

Despite Colt's careful planning and them taking care while they painted, he'd screwed up. Not Colt. Just him. He couldn't even remember how, but his dad had found something he wasn't happy with and knocked Reed around. His ribs ached for days. Closing his eyes, he tried to focus on something positive. Avery's smiling face as they danced at Halligan's materialized before him. Once he was in control again, he opened his eyes and reached into the sack at his feet. The plastic rustled as he searched for the scraper. He held the item out to Jess. "Tell you what—I'll tape around the windows and the trim while you go over the rough spots with the scraper."

As she accepted the tool, her huge grin tugged at his heart. "Thanks. That would be great."

"What's your favorite subject in school?" Reed asked as he tore off a strip of blue painter's tape and started taping around the window.

"I'm taking a creative-writing class and I like that a lot. I think that and computer programming are my favorites. Though I don't like them as much as I liked the website design class I took this summer."

"That's a really growing field, and it pays well. The guy I hired a couple of months ago to redo my company's site charged a fortune."

"Maybe I'll be good enough to help the next time your site needs updating," she added cheekily. "I'll even give you a family discount."

"It's a deal."

Reed's cell phone rang. When he answered the call, Ethan launched into a monologue on his difficulties with a product demonstration and how unreasonable the customer's demands were. From experience, Reed knew that until Ethan had vented, he wouldn't listen to anything else.

When the connection grew fuzzy, he walked around the yard searching for better reception. A minute later, Jess touched him on the arm. "Is everything okay? It's not about Dad, is it?"

He put his hand over his phone. "Don't worry. It's nothing serious, and it's not about your dad. It's work stuff."

The worry left her eyes, and her posture relaxed as she returned to scraping, while he returned his call. When it broke up again and the connection failed, he received a text from Ethan. "Urgent I speak to you on a decent phone line. Having problems. Can't fix. Need to send them to you so we can discuss."

He replied asking his vice president to check the shelter's website for a fax number and to send the information there, and said he'd call him from a landline.

"I need to go inside and get a fax. I'll only be a minute."

Jess smiled. "I'll be here."

AVERY SPOTTED REED'S TRUCK in the shelter parking lot when she returned from her meeting with Harper to discuss the information she'd compiled on other available properties. As Avery suspected, when she factored in remodeling an existing structure or building a new one, the cheaper properties turned out to be more costly, making purchasing their current property the best option. Now all they had to do was raise the sixty grand for the down payment. She shuddered. No matter how many times she heard the amount and told herself the goal was obtainable she still felt an initial flutter of panic.

Once inside, she checked in with the front-desk volunteer, Mrs. Russell, a former life-skills teacher who answered the shelter phones one afternoon a week. She and her black toy-poodle mix, Chandra, were practically Pet Walk legends when it came to the Best-Dressed Pet category.

"Anything I need to know about?"

"We've got everything under control."

"That doesn't surprise me in the least. I can't wait to see what you come up with for Chandra to wear at the Pet Walk this year."

The older woman smiled. "I've pulled out all the

stops but that's all I'm going to say. I don't want to ruin the surprise."

Avery told Mrs. Russell she'd be in her office working on the last details for the Pet Walk if anyone needed her. When she reached her door, she froze.

There sat Reed, all six foot two of him, looking enormous and even more masculine seated behind her ancient metal industrial desk. The hum of the fax machine on the stand by the door brought her back to earth.

"I thought you and Jess were painting outside this afternoon."

"We are. I just had something to take care of." He shifted in her chair, and it squeaked in protest. "How do you get any work done sitting in this rickety thing? It's damned uncomfortable, too. You need a chair that fits your position in the organization."

Was he serious? That's what he had to say when she found him making himself at home in *her* office? "I make do because the shelter can't afford new office furniture. The only way I'll get a new chair is if Santa puts one under the tree this Christmas."

What was she going to do with him here? An image of them rolling around on her desk appeared in her mind. As the heat raced up her neck into her face, she told herself she couldn't do that. At least not here.

When the fax machine quieted, he said, "Would you check to see if that's for me?"

She grabbed the paper, scanned the cover sheet and walked across the room. As she handed him the papers, she asked, "Why is someone sending you a fax here?"

"My VP's doing a customer demo, and he's having trouble. I texted him to fax the details to me so I can help him."

Wait a minute. If Reed was in here, where was Jess?

"Did you leave Jess alone outside? You're supposed to be supervising her."

"She'll be okay. She's not five."

"You don't get it. We have the policy regarding children under sixteen volunteering with a parent or guardian because of liability issues. I could get in trouble with the board."

"Help me out here. You know what it's like being in charge. Sometimes things go to hell."

How could she say no when he put it that way? She'd sound like an unreasonable tyrant. Why did Reed asking for favors as other volunteers often did get under her skin? Because something about him made her feel out of control.

"I need to make a quick call on a landline. My cell keeps dropping my calls. Would you mind if I used your phone?"

She gave him a tight-lipped smile. "By all means, my office is at your disposal."

He smiled openly as his gaze searched hers. "You always were a sport. Everyone can always count on you."

She grimaced. Yup, people could count on her and Old Faithful. That was just what a girl wanted to hear from a guy, especially a handsome ex. "Since you obviously missed it, I was being sarcastic."

"I didn't miss it. I ignored it."

That silly comment, said with the engaging smile she was so familiar with, made her grin. The man could charm his way out of the stickiest situation if he put his mind to the task.

"Go ahead. Read your fax. Make your call. I'll supervise Jess until you're done."

"Thanks, you're a pal."

Ouch. That comment hurt as much as *You always*

were a sport had. But wasn't that what she wanted? For Reed to see her as nothing more than a friend?

The words *Be careful what you wish for* taunted her as she stopped to get a bottle of water before she headed outside in search of Jess.

Why did Reed have to come back now when she was finally content with her life? The past few years had been tumultuous. Her father's death had shattered her world, leaving a huge void. Then her mother's cancer diagnosis had shaken her further. Now all she wanted to do was establish her career, settle into a routine and, she hoped, some time in the not-too-distant future find a man she could share her life with. Then Reed had swooped back into town, sending her flying around like a dry leaf in a strong autumn breeze.

She rounded the corner, spotted Jess and smiled. The teenager had almost as much paint on her clothes as she'd gotten on the wall. "You're doing a great job, but it looks like you'll have to do a second coat. I can still see the lettering."

She joined Jess and handed her the bottle of water. Why would someone paint *Animals shouldn't be in jail* on the shelter? "I know I asked before, but I'd really like to know. Do you know why whoever vandalized the shelter did it?"

"If I tell you, will you promise not to do anything about it?" Jess nervously fingered the water bottle's label. The plastic crackled in her hand.

Avery nodded. "I promise. The only reason I want to know is to make sure we don't have future problems."

"One of my friends let her dog out in the yard and forgot about him when she went out. The dog dug a hole under the fence and got loose. Animal control picked him up and brought him here. Her parents were pissed and made her pay them the money it cost to get him back."

"Thank you, I appreciate your honesty. I know your friend thinks it was terrible that she had to pay to get her dog back, but she was really lucky. A lot of times when a dog runs around loose we don't get a happy ending. Her dog could've gotten hit by a car because she was irresponsible."

"I really did tell her spray-painting the shelter wasn't a good idea," Jess added. "Can I ask you a question and you won't get mad?"

Avery considered stipulating as long as it didn't concern Reed, but decided the less she mentioned him the better. "Seems only fair."

"What's up with you and Uncle Reed?"

Such a simple question, but one so complicated to answer.

Avery considered tossing out a flippant comment or diverting Jess with another question, but that didn't seem right. Jess knew something was going on between her and Reed, or she wouldn't have asked.

"Your uncle and I have known each other since kindergarten. That makes it easy for us to push each other's buttons."

"My mom used to say that when a guy teases you or gives you a hard time it's because he likes you."

The mom who couldn't stick around had actually given Jess a worthwhile piece of advice? "I think that's true at your age, but it's different with adults."

"I don't know if I believe that."

That's my story and I'm sticking to it. "Reed and I really don't know each other anymore. He's changed a lot since he moved to California."

"You mean he wasn't always such a jerk?"

"He was always—" Avery paused, searching for the right word. Obviously things were still difficult between Jess and her uncle. She refused to make things worse by bad-mouthing him. "He's always been focused. In school he wasn't happy getting an A. He had to get the highest score in the class. He's trying with you. I know he loves you a lot. It's just that he's clueless about what to do."

"My dad was kinda that way when Mom died."

"But he got better, right?" After Jess nodded, Avery added, "Reed will, too."

Jess dunked the roller in paint and moved farther down the wall. "Did you two ever date?"

Avery froze, trying to decide how to respond to the awkward question. *Dated* hardly described their past relationship. He was her first love. The first man she'd imagined spending her life with.

"Yes, we did, but we broke up when we went to college."

"I think he still likes you."

No, Jess, don't say that. Anything but that.

Avery almost asked, *Really, you think so?*

Lord, I've been transported back to junior high. She remembered how she and her friends speculated about what guys liked what girls. Next thing she'd be asking Jess if Reed talked about her and what he said.

"Surely he's got a girlfriend in California."

The roller stopped. Paint dripped onto the grass at Jess's feet as she stared at Avery.

Now I've done it. She thinks I like him, too.

"If he's got a girlfriend, they don't talk very much." Jess resumed painting. "He's on the phone all the time, but it doesn't ever sound like he's talking about anything but business."

That answer left Avery far happier than it should have. She had to end this conversation before that gleam in Jess's eyes got any brighter.

"Hey, what are you two talking about?"

Avery glanced over her shoulder and spotted Reed walking toward them. "We're talking about how attached you are to your phone."

Jess laughed. "You're on the phone more than anyone I know."

As he strode toward them, looking so sexy and confident, Avery realized how easy it would be to care for him again. She had to get out of here while she still possessed a sliver of willpower. "I'll leave you to finish up here. I'm off to see who I can tap for a donation."

Coward, the little voice inside her taunted as she walked away.

THAT NIGHT AS REED AND JESS cleaned up after dinner he said, "Were you and Avery really talking about how much I'm on the phone?"

"And other stuff. She said we'll need to put another coat of paint on the wall." Jess picked up a plate and placed it in the dishwasher.

"We can take care of that tomorrow afternoon. Did she say anything else? Anything about me?" Right after the words left his mouth, he cringed. Living with a teenager was rotting his brain. He sounded like a lovestruck tenth grader.

Before Jess could answer the oven timer went off. He went to shut it off, and noticed the oven wasn't on. "What's the timer for?"

"Dad said I could Skype him at six o'clock tonight."

He waved toward the door. "Go. I'll finish cleaning up. Tell your dad I said hello."

"I will." Jess tossed the words over her shoulder as she darted out of the room.

The kitchen back in order, Reed returned to his room and booted up his laptop. There was a message from his lawyer waiting in his inbox. Surprisingly, threatening to go public with Colt's story had failed to change the association's stance, forcing his lawyer to contact the media. Apparently a reporter, Sylvia Parsons from WTLV, First Coast News in Jacksonville, was waiting for his call. Reed glanced at his watch, adjusted for the time difference and figured since it was only eight in Florida, he might as well call now.

"I heard about your niece's situation, but I wanted to talk with you to see if the story is something we'd be interested in featuring," Sylvia said in a smooth, made-for-TV voice. "I have to admit I'm a little confused. Since you're able to stay with her in Colorado, why do you need the association to make an exception for your niece to live with her grandparents?"

She needs to stay with them because I'm incompetent. I'll mess things up so bad she'll spend the rest of her life on a therapist's couch processing the nightmare.

"My brother's original plan was that his in-laws would come to Colorado if he were deployed. Unfortunately, his mother in-law recently broke her hip and needs to stay close to her doctors. Because I'm a bachelor, I was the backup plan. What do I know about raising children?" He paused and tried to loosen up. He sounded as dry as a corporate annual report. He needed to get Sylvia to step into Jess's shoes. "Think back to when you were fourteen. Can you imagine living with your bachelor uncle?"

The reporter laughed. "Are you saying dealing with a teenager is tough?"

"Don't get me wrong. My niece is wonderful, but Jess would be much better off living with her grandparents. They've raised a child. They're better equipped to nurture and guide her. Jess needs the stability they can provide."

A moment passed and then Sylvia said, "This is exactly the kind of human-interest story our viewers want to hear about. I'll contact your niece's grandparents and the association for their take on the issue. May I call you if I have further questions after I speak with them?"

"Please do."

Sylvia ended the call by thanking him for his time and said she'd let him know when they planned to air the story.

Reed guessed it would never make it to air because the association would buckle after talking to the reporter. No one wanted to look as if they weren't supporting the country's servicemen and women and their families.

Maybe the day hadn't been a total loss after all. Jess would be better off with her grandparents, and he could return to his life and his business. That was good news. Wasn't it?

Chapter Seven

Since Reed and Jess had finished painting the exterior wall the day before, today would be their first day as official volunteers, and Avery was out to set Reed straight. Again, yesterday, he'd strolled into her office to make business calls, send faxes and use her computer. Each time he assured her he'd be only a couple of minutes, and somehow he'd left her feeling that she couldn't tell him no.

Today would be different. She'd be firm but polite. The shelter's fund-raiser was only weeks away and she couldn't concentrate on her work with him popping in and out of her office like a Whac-A-Mole. She'd also make it clear that now that he was an actual volunteer, she expected him to give the shelter his full attention, unless a genuine, bona fide emergency came up at his company.

When the pair arrived, she greeted them as she would any other volunteers on their first day, ignoring how great Reed looked in his worn jeans, tight Stanford T-shirt and his cowboy boots. She ran through the shelter rules and then paused and looked at Reed. "When you're here, I expect your full attention to be on what you're doing. That means, unless it's something that absolutely can't wait, we prefer you not make any personal calls. Are we clear on that?"

"Got it," Reed replied, though she could see in his gaze that he was already distracted.

"So what do you want us doing today?" Jess asked.

"I'll give you a choice. You can either clean the kennels or the cat boxes or bathe the dogs. What'll it be?" She bit her lip to keep from smiling as she waited for Reed's reaction.

She felt a twinge of guilt at asking him and Jess to do some of the less pleasant jobs, but the shelter was like any other business: those with seniority got the plum assignments.

"That's your idea of a choice? Haven't you heard of assessing volunteer strengths and assigning them tasks that best utilize their skills?" While his expression remained calm, a note of distaste crept into his voice. "Don't you have anything more managerial that needs to be done? Or maybe we could walk the dogs?"

She knew his type. He thought volunteering at the shelter would be a sweet gig that consisted of playing with kittens and walking dogs. He was one of those volunteers who turned squeamish or arrogant when it came to the less desirable tasks that needed to be done.

"You haven't even been volunteering five minutes, and you're questioning me." Avery paused, shoved her hands into her pockets, and struggled to control her rising frustration. She dealt with opinionated volunteers all the time and had developed a great repertoire of phrases to gently get her point across without offending anyone. She could manage him—and she could build a rocket ship in her spare time and fly to the moon for her next vacation, too.

"I'm sure you have some great ideas on how you

could help the shelter, but the new manager at the Pet Palace is stopping by tomorrow morning. If he likes what he sees, the company could become a generous sponsor for the Pet Walk. That means today everyone's working on getting the animals and the shelter looking their best. *Everyone's* cleaning."

Reed turned to his niece, his arms crossed over his broad chest. "No way am I cleaning cat boxes."

"What do we have to do to clean the kennels?" Jess asked.

"You scoop up the poop and hose them down." Avery sneaked a peek at Reed.

His eyes widened and his jaw tightened for a minute before he regained his control. Avery bit the inside of her lip to keep from laughing. Turning the tables on him and issuing orders could become her favorite pastime.

"That doesn't sound great, either," Reed snapped. "How about we sweep and dust the place?"

Avery opened her mouth to give Reed a lecture on who was in charge at the shelter but stopped. You'd think she and Reed were the two teenagers the way they jockeyed for control.

"What is it with you two?" Jess waved her hand between the adults, and her irritation slammed into Avery. "In the interest of world peace, I'm choosing. We're bathing dogs today. I bathe Thor all the time." The teenager faced her uncle, shaking her index finger at him. "If you say one word about it, Uncle Reed, we'll clean cat boxes, and I'll make you scoop the poop."

"I guess she told us." Avery laughed, relieved that the teenager had broken the tension. How did Reed so easily get on her nerves?

"Bathing dogs it is," Reed said.

Avery motioned for Reed and Jess to follow her. "Let me show you the grooming room."

She gave them a quick tour of the rest of the offices, as well as the dog kennels and cat area, and then she took them inside a small room that housed plenty of cupboards, a refrigerator and a large metal tub. "One of our dog-walker volunteers will bring in a dog."

Avery explained the process, how to work the sprayer and where towels were located. Then she asked if they had any questions.

"Jess and I can handle it. How hard can it be?" Reed flashed her a confident smile.

Avery bit her lip. She couldn't wait to hear what he had to say in twenty minutes when he was drenched and covered in fur. Avery pointed to the plastic aprons hanging on pegs along the wall. "You'll want to put one of those on. It'll keep you from getting completely soaked. I'll check back in a while. Wish me luck. I'm talking to the head of Griffin's network to ask for a donation."

"What's your strategy?" Reed asked.

"I'm going to tell him about the shelter, our current problem and ask for a donation." What did he think she was going to do? Call up a network executive, chat with him for a minute and then ask him to make cookies for the bake sale they planned to have next month?

He shook his head, as if she'd committed some ridiculous mistake like going into Starbucks and ordering soda. "That's not a plan for success."

Avery noticed Jess's fist clenched around the apron she held. Her gaze darted back and forth between the adults. *She's waiting for round two to start.* Jess's life didn't need any more turmoil. "Jess, will you go see Emma, my volunteer coordinator? Her office is next to mine. Tell her I said she's to take you to meet Mrs. Hartman. She'll be bringing dogs to you to bathe."

After glancing between the two adults again, probably to make sure they wouldn't come to blows while she was gone, Jess left.

"We have to find a way to get along," Avery said once the door closed.

"I thought we got along pretty well the other night at Halligan's."

Reed's harsh expression left no doubt about what he meant. Heat raced through her. She crossed her arms over her chest, trying to channel the energy darting through her body into confidence.

The other night was a mistake. She couldn't force the words past the lump in her throat. Despite knowing better, she couldn't think of what had happened between them that way. Not when she'd felt alive in a way she hadn't in years. "That was a social setting. This is my business. I can't have volunteers questioning every decision I make."

"I asked a couple of questions. What's the big deal?"

SHE WANTED TO PROVE she was in charge. Reed should've realized that the moment he walked in the door today. The challenging gleam in her eye when she'd offered him the unappetizing choice of tasks had been the first tip-off. Then she'd stood there and explained how to wash a dog, as if it was rocket science and he was a grade-school kid.

Anyone could handle washing a dog. Get the dog wet. Throw on the shampoo. Scrub. Rinse. Simple.

"I'm used to being in charge. Taking orders has never sat well with me." Part of the baggage his father had left him with.

"Can't you see how much it bothers Jess when you do that? Did her parents fight a lot before her mom left?"

Had Colt's marriage been like their parents', where the fights rattled the rafters and occurred more often than the weather changed? He remembered how those fights had left him with knots in his stomach and scared to leave his room for fear of what he'd find.

He hadn't considered how his and Avery's disagreements would affect Jess. He hadn't seen them as any big deal. He should've realized his niece would see them differently, but he hadn't. How did Avery always see what he missed? Again, he'd been clueless, while Avery understood. Just another example of what a lousy father he'd be.

"I don't know much about Colt's marriage. He never talked about it, but things can't have been too good. She was having an affair and ran off."

"I'm worried that us not getting along reminds her of what happened between her parents."

Reed remembered how he and his brother had felt as they hid in their room trying to block out the angry words that their parents hurled at each other. But his situation with Avery wasn't the same. They weren't married. Still, there was definitely something between them. Something strong that they both fought against, and damned if he knew what to do about it. But he could keep Jess from getting caught in the crossfire.

"What's going on with us? We never used to argue like this." He shoved his hands into his pockets, uncertain of how to continue.

"We're different people than we were in high school." Avery resisted the urge to pick at her fingernail. "I care about Jess, and I don't want our disagreements to hurt her. I'll make an effort to go easier on you, if you'll work on questioning my decisions less."

He nodded. "It may not have seemed like it, but I want to help. I just went about it the wrong way. I thought I could give you a new perspective on approaching executives for donations. Charities ask me for money all the time. To convince a major corporate player to write you a big check you have to tell him what it'll do for his business."

"This isn't the first time I've done this."

"Small-business owners are more tied to the community than major national corporate types. Why should a global company care about a little animal shelter in Estes Park?"

"Because the host of one of their most popular reality shows cares about it."

He stepped toward her, not sure of what he intended to do, but needing to erase the censure on her face. "Why won't you let me help you where I can do the most good?"

He wasn't sure what he'd done, but he'd made another mistake. Just as he'd done with Jess. What was the deal? He'd never had this much trouble with women before.

"What makes you think you can breeze in here after all these years and give me advice? Worry about your own life. Mine's off-limits." Though her voice remained level and calm, her irritation came through loud and clear.

Her words cut through him. His own life? What did his consist of? He had his business. Nothing else, except for a brother and a niece he saw briefly on major holidays. Other than Colt and Jess, who would care if he stepped into the street tomorrow and got hit by a bus?

That was the way he'd chosen since he left Estes Park. Why did the fact sour his stomach now?

Because Avery saw him and his life as lacking, and pitied him for it.

Instead of addressing her comment, he turned the conversation back to fund-raising. "When you call these executives, don't ask them if they want to donate. Give them a number and ask if you can count on them for that amount."

Before Avery could respond, the door opened and Jess returned with a scraggly, wire-haired dog of an indeterminate color. "Mrs. Hartman said to keep a close eye on Baxter because he's an escape artist."

Avery strolled over to the dog and scratched him behind the ear. "He's been known to wiggle out of his collar."

"She also told me the people who adopted him returned him," Jess said, her face filled with concern. "She said he was here for months before."

"He kept getting out of the backyard. The couple who adopted him wanted an outside dog. Baxter wasn't a good fit for them." Avery scratched the mutt under his chin. "We just have to find the right family."

"With that face? Good luck."

"That's mean, Uncle Reed," Jess said as she patted the dog. "Looks aren't everything."

He nodded toward the animal. "He'd better hope someone else thinks that, too."

"He'll be a loyal companion to whoever earns his trust." Avery glared at Reed as if he'd said her baby was ugly. Then she glanced at her watch. "I've got to go. I have to make that call."

After Avery left, Reed turned to Jess. "Since you're the one with experience, you're in charge."

Reed crossed the room and looked down at the mutt standing beside his niece. Instead of growling like Thor, Baxter looked up, wagged his rat tail and then yawned. "You're not fooling me with the tame routine, buddy. I've been warned about you."

"I agree with Avery." Jess scratched the dog behind his floppy big ears. "There's something about him. How could they give up on him after only a week?"

Reed slipped his arm under the dog's belly and lifted him into the metal tub. "He's got a street-smart look to him. He'll be fine."

"What if no one else wants him?"

Reed didn't have to be a trained therapist to realize there was more going on here than Jess worrying about this stray. But that didn't mean he knew what to do about it. "You've got more than this mutt on your mind. Want to talk about it?"

Jess reached for the leash attached to the tub, hooked it to the dog's collar and then turned on the water. "I heard on the news that some soldiers were killed in Afghanistan." When her voice cracked, she bit her lip and paused.

"I'm worried about him, too. That's why every time I talk to him I remind him to be careful."

Jess's lip quivered. "Sometimes that's not enough. People get hurt over there every day."

He put his arm around her shoulder. "We'll just have to pray that he stays safe."

"What if Dad doesn't come home? I won't have anyone."

Her pain reached inside him and squeezed the heart he hadn't been sure he still possessed. He and Jess were so alike. Both alone and determined to hide the fact. "You'll have me."

Jess eyed him as if she wasn't sure if she believed him but couldn't bring herself to voice the words. Not that he blamed her. What had he done to earn her trust?

"I mean it. You can count on me. You and your dad are the only family I have. Being the older brother, he saw me through some tough times when I was a kid." How many times had Colt hauled him away when things got too heated between him and his father? If it hadn't been for his brother, Reed probably would've beaten the hell out of his father much sooner, or his father would've killed him for trying. "There's nothing I wouldn't do for him, and the same is true for you."

The rush of water on metal and the chug as it swirled down the drain filled the awkward silence between them. As what he'd said hung between them, Reed realized he meant every word. Then the dog nudged Jess.

"Okay, boss, what do we need to do first?" Reed asked.

Jess waved her hand under the water and used the sprayer to douse the animal. The unmistakable smell of wet dog wafted through the air. "Quick, hand me the shampoo."

After Reed handed her the squirt bottle with *shampoo* written on it in purple marker. Jess poured a generous amount of liquid into her palm and scrubbed the dog.

Reed's phone dinged, indicating a text, but remembering what Avery had said about remaining focused on shelter business, he ignored the message. Two more pings came in quick succession, followed by his phone ringing. "Since you've got things under control, do you mind if I check my phone?"

"I don't know." Jess dumped more shampoo into her

palm. "Avery said we shouldn't take any calls unless it's an emergency."

"I won't know if it's important until I check my messages."

"Okay, but if we get in trouble, you're on your own."

Reed pulled up the message. The dog shifted, and Reed guessed the mutt was about to shower them by shaking. Not wanting to get sprayed, he stepped a few feet away.

"Uncle Reed, I need your help."

He glanced at Jess as he shoved his phone into his pocket. The dog twisted and turned, trying to squirm out of his collar. Jess reached for the dog, trying to yank the collar back down and get the dog under control. Before Reed reached them, Baxter wiggled free. Jess lunged for the dog, but he ducked under her arms and jumped out of the tub. "Catch him, Uncle Reed!"

Reed raced forward, putting himself between the door and the dog. Baxter stopped. As he reached for the dog, the animal shook itself, spraying shampoo-laced water everywhere, including in Reed's face. Eyes stinging from the soap, he managed to wrap his arms around the dog.

The mutt licked his face and squirmed against him. "Great. This dog likes me." As Jess rushed toward him, he called out, "Slow down. The floor's wet."

Before he finished his warning, she started slipping and sliding. He reached for her, and the dog bolted out the door.

After regaining their balance, he and Jess raced out after the escapee, but all Reed could think about was how Avery would think he was a complete ass. That was, if she didn't kill him.

THOUGH AVERY WOULDN'T ADMIT the truth under any form of torture, what Reed had said about soliciting donations made sense, and she decided to implement his suggestion with the network executive Griffin had told her to contact. After a minute of small talk, mostly centered on Griffin and Maggie's daughter, Michaela, Avery asked the man to commit to a five-thousand-dollar donation.

His response—that he'd be happy to—combined with her excitement almost knocked her out of her chair. "That's wonderful. I can't tell you how much I appreciate your generous donation."

Five thousand dollars was beyond generous, and more than doubled the amount any one sponsor had donated last year.

Frenzied voices bounced through the shelter. Something was wrong. Avery knew the sound of chaos when she heard it. She wrapped up her call before whatever mess had developed descended on her. That was the last thing she wanted a man who'd agreed to donate five thousand dollars to hear.

She'd no sooner ended her call when a soaking-wet Baxter charged past her office, a trail of bubbles floating behind him. As she headed for her door, she shouted, "Keep all the doors closed. Baxter's loose."

Not good. What had gone wrong? She barreled out of her office and ran into something solid. Strong arms wrapped around her as she fell. Glancing upward, she recognized Reed a second before they hit the unyielding tile floor with him under her.

"Guess bathing dogs was harder than you thought." Instead of her voice sounding critical, the words came out in a husky rush. All she could think about was his hard body under hers. Her body tingled with excitement as she rolled off him.

"That dog's a menace." Reed stood beside her, his shirt damp and clinging to his muscled frame.

As she worked to keep her breathing even and regain control, she straightened her top, refusing to look at him. When he held her all she could think about was how right it felt to be in them.

"Baxter's like you. He wants things his way, doesn't take direction well and is hard to teach."

"Touché. You can't teach an old dog new tricks."

"Yes, you can. It's all a matter of giving him the right incentive and encouragement."

"That applies to males in general."

No way was she going there with him. Flipping a switch inside her head, Avery slipped back into director mode, hoping that would calm her raging hormones. "What happened? How did bathing a dog turn into a prison break?"

"Avery, he's headed your way," Emma shouted from somewhere. Seconds later, Baxter bounded down the hallway.

"Stop," Reed commanded.

Avery stared openmouthed as the dog skidded to a halt at Reed's feet.

"I'm sorry, Avery." A breathless Jess materialized beside them, a leash and collar dangling from her fingertips, which she immediately slipped on the dog. "I thought I had Baxter under control, but by the time I realized I needed help and called out to Uncle Reed and he got off the phone—"

"Jess, take Baxter back to the bathing room," Avery said, her voice and her entire body tight.

Her temper had reached its limit. She couldn't take this. She couldn't handle Reed being here at the shelter. So much weighed on her. She needed order at work right now, and Reed had thrown her entire life into a state of chaos.

Once Jess and the dog were out of sight, Avery whirled around to face Reed. "I asked you to give your work here at the shelter your full attention. I told you how important it was that we get the animals and the shelter cleaned up for the visit tomorrow. What was it this time? What was so important that you were on the phone instead of concentrating on what you were doing here?"

When he started to answer, she waved her hand in the air to halt him. "Never mind. I don't want to hear it. I'm done. Jess can still volunteer here, but I don't want you to come back. You may not take what we do here seriously, but we do. I can't have someone screwing things up for us, especially now." She knew she was overreacting, but she couldn't help it. "Do you know what this would've looked like to the Pet Palace manager? It would look like I don't have control of the situation."

Which she didn't whenever Reed was within twenty feet of her.

"You can't tell me things always go according to plan," he countered.

The arrogance in his gaze only fueled her anger. "No, they don't, but if you can't put the shelter first, I don't want you here."

Screw the shelter's policy regarding student volunteers. She'd figure something out to help Jess continue volunteering and complete her community service, but she couldn't take Reed invading her work environment any longer. She started to walk away.

"Wait a minute, Avery. Let me explain."

She glanced over her shoulder at Reed. He stood there, his hands shoved into his jeans pockets, his gaze pleading, but she didn't care. It was too little, too late. "Nothing you can say will change my mind. I'll drop Jess off on my way home. Now leave. After all, that's what you're good at."

Chapter Eight

After driving Jess home, Avery returned to the shelter and headed straight for Emma's office. Thankful to find her friend still there, she sank into the corner armchair, but then jumped up again and started pacing. "Can you believe what Reed did today? He's driving me crazy. How can everything he does push my buttons? And how dare he come in here and give me advice about soliciting donations, like he knows anything about working for a nonprofit agency?"

"Calm down, because if you don't, I'm going to make you hold a puppy in order to lower your blood pressure before you stroke out."

Avery laughed as she collapsed into the chair across from her friend. "Is that your way of saying I've gone off the deep end?"

"I've never seen you like this before."

"I've never had an ex-boyfriend invade my work life before."

"You sure things are over with Reed? When you two were dancing at Halligan's the other night, I almost ran for a fire extinguisher things got so hot. When was the last time you felt that kind of heat with a guy?"

A couple of her past relationships had come close, at

least in the beginning, but the chemistry never lasted with anyone. Except Reed.

"Somewhere along the way you forgot about having a life."

"I have one." She had her family. A challenging job. Okay, right now it was too challenging, but it was a good job. She had friends. So she didn't have a love life right now. A woman couldn't have it all, all the time.

But that didn't keep her from wanting it all. She dreamed of finding a relationship like her parents had had. One where they were best friends and lovers. One where he made her laugh and stood by her during the tough times. With someone who would give her children. Something Reed would never do.

"Let me amend that. You forgot about having a love life," Emma shot back. "You need to find a guy you're attracted to and sleep with him."

If only the problem could be solved that easily.

"That's not my style." Avery picked a long white dog hair off her jeans. "I want more than that."

Her friend shook her head. "I know. You're a soul-mate kind of gal. Personally, I don't see what's wrong with being happy with someone just for right now."

Avery refused to settle. If she did, she knew eventually she'd resent her decision, and that emotion would sour the relationship. Realizing those two things had been what had finally helped her move on after Reed. "You're right. I should be happy right now."

Avery stared at her friend and took a deep breath. "I threw Reed out and told him not to come back. The question is how we keep people from finding out Jess is volunteering here without a parent or guardian supervising her."

Panic flared in Emma's eyes. "We can't. It's impossible to keep a secret in this town, and we've got two of the biggest gossips for volunteers. You have to let Reed come back. If you don't, I'll be inundated with requests from other parents for us to make an exception for their kids." Emma laughed. "I can see the headlines now. Volunteer Director of the Estes Park Animal Shelter Admitted to Psych Ward After Being Driven Insane by Unruly Preteen Volunteers."

"I can't have him here." Avery's body ached from the pain having Reed back in town dredged up. While her family knew Reed had broken up with her via email, no one knew the whole story. She started telling Emma about her past with Reed, and soon everything tumbled out. Every agonizing detail she'd held on to for too long.

Her hands clutched together in her lap, Avery peered at her friend. "I can't see my life without someday having children."

"He's been gone a long time. Maybe he's changed his mind about kids."

"I can't take the risk. I hurt so bad the last time. I can't go through that again." Tears stung Avery's eyes.

"Well, then, he's out." Emma's matter-of-fact attitude eased Avery's fears. "All we have to do is find someone other than a staff person to supervise Jess. If my mom wasn't so allergic to animal dander, I'd ask her to help us out."

Avery smiled, latching on to the answer. "I've got the perfect solution. I'll ask my mom."

The only problem was how to get her mother to agree without letting her know why she really didn't want Reed around.

THE NEXT DAY, AS REED SAT at the desk in Colt's office trying to focus on the spreadsheet in front of him, he still couldn't believe he'd gotten fired from a volunteer job. He'd never been fired from anything before.

Leave. After all, that's what you're good at.

Maybe Avery throwing him out was for the best. Common sense insisted that was the case, but he'd still picked up his phone more than once to call her. Damn, he'd created more than a little chaos yesterday. He considered sending her flowers, but she wasn't big on stuff like that. She valued actions. She'd tell him unless he changed his behavior, he'd wasted his money. He needed to make things up to her, wanted to prove she was wrong, that business wasn't all that mattered to him.

Making things right. That's what counted with Avery, but how could he do that?

The shelter. He could make a donation.

He did a Google search and located the Estes Park animal shelter's website. The first thing he noticed was that the site took too long to load and looked amateurish. The colors were hard on the eyes. The pictures looked like stock photos. It was poorly organized and not very user friendly.

He had trouble locating information on the Pet Walk, and when he did click on the link, there was no mention of the shelter's precarious financial situation, but he did locate a donation link. However, once he got there, he had to navigate past numerous screens. With his finger resting on the mouse about to click Submit, he stopped. Making a donation wasn't any different than sending flowers. It took no effort, no work. Lip service. That's what Avery would say.

Curious about how Avery's site compared to others, he searched more animal-shelter sites. As he went, he bookmarked the ones he liked, and jotted down notes.

He really had wanted to help yesterday, but he'd ended up doing the opposite. She'd been right. All he'd thought about was his business, feeling his problems trumped hers in importance. Looking back now, he recognized the strain that clouded her usually bright blue eyes. The shelter's financial situation had to be wearing on her.

The shelter was a business. Avery's business. Logically he'd known that, but somewhere in practice, he'd forgotten the fact. He was a volunteer expected to do a job—whatever Avery, or any other staff member, decided needed to be done.

He'd been an arrogant bastard, and as a result he'd caused problems for Avery.

She'd been right to throw his sorry ass out.

The alarm on his phone went off, reminding him to leave to pick up Jess from the shelter. As he drove through town and waited in the parking lot for his niece, a plan on how he could make amends with Avery started forming.

"How did volunteering go today? Is Avery still mad at me?" he asked when Jess climbed into the truck.

"I don't know because we didn't talk about you. You were really a jerk. How would you like it if someone came into your company and questioned everything you told them to do?"

"I know. I want to do something for Avery, but I need your help."

Jess tilted her head and stared at him skeptically. "Why should I help you? What's in it for me?"

"If you do, I'll give you your phone back."

"What about computer privileges?"

"You're pushing it."

"Then you're on your own. Avery's not mad at me."

Damn. Jess had him over a barrel, and they both knew it. "Deal. I want to put together a marketing proposal for the shelter and develop an updated website to show Avery. Maybe create a plan for Twitter, Facebook and Pinterest to increase visibility there, too."

As they made their way back to the ranch, he smiled as they passed Swanson's Ice Cream Shop where he and Avery had shared more hot fudge sundaes than he could count, and McCabe's Pizza, another favorite hangout. Not all his memories were bad.

He and Jess talked about options for the website. When they arrived home they headed into Colt's office. Reed moved the leather armchair closer to the desk for Jess and then settled into the desk chair. They spent the next half hour checking out other shelter websites.

Avery had been right about Jess, too. He needed to make an effort to find out who his niece was. Instead, he'd shown up, been preoccupied with his own problems and expected her to fall in line. Working together on the website could be a good start to fixing that problem.

An image of him decades from now taunted him. His business days behind him, he sat alone in a retirement home staring at a picture of his niece and her family that he'd gotten in her last Christmas card. One he cherished as his only connection with family.

Was that what he really wanted?

"I don't know if I'm good enough to design a website for a real business," Jess said, pulling Reed away from his thoughts.

"We can give it a shot. I picked up a lot from the consultant who updated my company website a few months ago."

"If we have problems, I could contact my summer-school instructor."

"That's a great idea." He pulled up the Estes Park animal shelter website. "Look at this."

Jess shuddered. "That's scary bad. That red is awful, and the rest of the site is too dark. It needs happy colors. Soft ones that make people feel all warm and fuzzy inside."

"You have a good eye." He pulled up another shelter's website. "The most important thing for the shelter right now is raising money, but there's nothing on their site about how bad the situation is. This one has a graph showing how close they are to their fund-raising goal."

"That's cool. We should add something like that."

He jotted down her suggestion on the paper to his right before he returned to the site. "The information on the Pet Walk's buried way down here." Reed scrolled down the page. "We also need to simplify the online donation process."

Jess nodded. Then she tilted her head and smiled. "I know why you're doing this. Avery told me you two used to date. You've got the hots for her. You're hoping if you do all this stuff she won't be mad, and she'll go out with you."

Reed told himself he didn't have ulterior motives, and even if he did, Avery wouldn't be easily swayed.

Every day, Avery crept into his thoughts more. Seeing her, being with her made being back bearable. Life in Estes Park was a lot more fun when he was with Avery.

"That's not it. I'm doing this because I messed up. Part of being responsible is making up for what I did. Since Avery won't let me back in the building, this is one way I can do that. Plus, the shelter provides a valuable community service. I want to help them raise the money they need."

"That's so lame, and you're such a liar."

That might be true, but he'd never admit it.

THAT NIGHT AS AVERY and her mom stood in the kitchen making spaghetti and meatballs, Avery chatted about her day, intent on working up to the subject of her mom supervising Jess. "I spoke to the bigwig at Griffin's network today. He agreed to donate five thousand dollars. I'm starting to believe we can raise the money for the down payment."

"I have every faith in you."

Still not ready to broach the real issue, Avery told her mom about the Pet Palace manager's visit. "I'm hoping they'll agree to be one of our sponsors for the Pet Walk. It's really been a hassle moving up the event, but if we didn't, we'd never raise the money in time."

Her mom stopped stirring the sauce and glanced at Avery, her brow furrowed. "How about you get to the point?"

"And here I thought I was being subtle. I should've known I couldn't put anything over on you." Avery grabbed a deep breath and chose her words carefully. "Jess Montgomery's supposed to be volunteering at the shelter to fulfill her court-ordered community service, but Reed's too busy managing the ranch and seeing to his own business. He doesn't have time to supervise her, but I can't overlook our rule about kids under sixteen needing an adult chaperone."

Avery bit her lip. She sounded as if she was twelve and trying to divert her mom from the real issue by laying the situation out in one long recitation. "I was hoping you'd be willing to volunteer with Jess and supervise her."

Her mom turned and slowly crossed her arms over

her chest. The look she leveled on Avery clearly stated Nannette McAlister knew good and well her daughter was trying to put a hat on a pig. "You said you can't put anything over on me, so why did you try spinning that tale when you knew I'd see right through it?" Her gaze softened. "What really happened between you and Reed? And keep in mind, I heard how cozy you were at Halligan's."

"Who told you, and what did you hear?"

"Griffin said you two were dancing so close *he* was embarrassed."

Avery winced. With her brother's past, her mom probably imagined she and Reed had been seconds away from tearing off each other's clothes and doing the deed in the middle of the dance floor. With no option left but the truth, Avery said, "Reed's driving me crazy at the shelter, Mom." At the shelter? Reed was driving her just plain crazy. "Every time I tell him what to do, he suggests what he should do instead, and he's on the phone constantly with his work." Avery explained about the Baxter incident. "I can't have that kind of disorder at the shelter right now. I have so much to worry about already."

"You should work this out with him."

No way. Every time she saw Reed she lost her common sense, her temper or her self-control. No matter what happened, things didn't go well. Being around Reed was like being the only person at work without a cold. Even with constant hand washing, sooner or later, the bug worked its way past her immune system.

"I know, but now isn't the time. Not when I've got all I can handle keeping the shelter open. Once the Pet Walk's over, and we've got the loan, then I can cope with Reed." She prayed she'd slide this little white lie past her mom. If she did, she'd never tell another one.

Her mom reached out and brushed her cheek. "Of course I'll help you."

"Despite what Griffin said, Reed and I aren't getting back together. It's too late for that. Promise me you won't play matchmaker."

"The thought never crossed my mind, and even if it had, doing that would be as productive as planting my garden in January. I learned early on that you kids have minds of your own."

"Thanks, Mom," she said, praying that her mother stuck to her word.

"That boy had a rough life growing up. He didn't have the advantage of having wonderful parents like you did."

Avery kissed her mother on the cheek. "You're right about that." She paused and then asked a question she'd often wondered about. "Why didn't anyone ever call child welfare on Reed's dad?"

"Your dad and I never knew Aaron Montgomery was physically abusing his sons until that night Reed showed up at our door with that awful bruise on his face. As far as I know, no one knew how bad things were for those boys. They never told anyone, and no one ever saw marks on them. Their father saw to that."

"I don't understand why Reed never told me."

Nannette turned off the stove, and walked to the kitchen table with Avery following her. Once settled, she clasped her daughter's hand. "Reed and his brother always were proud. When their mother died, their father refused everyone's offers of help. Those boys worked so hard to take care of themselves. How would you have acted if he had told you?"

"I'd have supported him. I'd have helped him however I could have."

"How would he have seen your reaction?"

As pity.

"That boy has been running for years. It can't be easy for Reed being back in that house with the memories he has of the place," her mother continued.

"This isn't the first time he's been back."

But now that Avery thought about it, when he'd visited Colt and Jess over the past years, no one had mentioned seeing him in town. The only way anyone knew Reed had been there was because Colt told them.

"No, but this time he's staying longer than a weekend, and now everyone knows what his life was like growing up. I said I wouldn't play matchmaker, and I won't, but I will say you could do a lot worse than Reed Montgomery."

Before Avery could respond, the back door opened and in walked Griffin and Maggie. Griffen cradled Michaela in his arms. Avery's heart ached. Her mother wouldn't say she could do a lot worse than Reed if she knew what Avery would have to give up to be with him.

THE NEXT FEW DAYS WENT BY in a blur for Avery. She lined up vendors for the Pet Walk. She met with the local media about the shelter's predicament and the date change for the Pet Walk. Volunteers updated the signs and posters around the town. They'd called and emailed every registered participant. She'd spayed or neutered the latest batch of adoptable animals and attended to an injured horse they'd received when his owner abandoned him.

Her life was running smoothly again. Each night she fell into bed exhausted but satisfied with what she'd accomplished, and she'd started to believe the shelter would reach its sixty-thousand-dollar goal.

And she hadn't seen Reed since she'd thrown him out of the shelter.

When he arrived to pick up Jess, he waited in the parking lot. What had she expected? That he'd pick Jess up one day, wander into her office and fall at her feet to apologize?

Nannette's laughter floated through the air a second before she and Jess entered the office. "Avery, did you know Jess is a budding author? She let me read a piece for school she wrote about the shelter. I told her she needed to show it to you."

"I know you're busy. You don't have to read it, but I got an A on the assignment." Pride shone on Jess's face as she clutched the paper in her hand.

Avery's heart melted. This young girl was eager to please and desperate for attention, while so afraid she'd disappoint. The woman hadn't deserved this wonderful child. "I'd love to read what you wrote."

As Jess walked across the room and handed Avery the paper, she marveled at the changes in the teenager since she'd started volunteering at the shelter, and especially since she'd been with Nannette. Jess had blossomed. The sullen, angry teen was gone and she'd started making new friends. Apparently she'd finally realized friends who threw her under the bus weren't the best kind to have.

Once Avery had read Jess's paper on the value animal shelters provided for society, she said, "This is amazing. You've really captured the heart of what we do here."

"Tell her your idea," Nannette coaxed.

"I noticed no one's written a blog entry for the shelter in a while," Jess said.

Avery winced. Blogging was yet another aspect of the director's position she loathed. The board had brought up the subject in their last meeting, emphasizing the growing importance of social media and how they were woefully behind the times. From their expectations and her expanding job description, they must think she had twenty-eight hours in her day. "So I've been told recently by the board. It's on my to-do list, but I'll admit it's at the bottom."

"I could write one about the animals who need to be adopted, and what we do here at the shelter. It's important work, but people don't realize we do more than find homes for strays."

"I think that's a great idea. I'll have to approve your blog before they go online."

Jess nodded, her brown hair falling in her face. "I thought we could link it with our Facebook page, which needs work, too, by the way."

That was the story of Avery's life lately and everything she did—needs work, under reconstruction. "Let's see how the blog goes first. We can use your paper as the first one. I appreciate your help. You've got great ideas and tons of enthusiasm, but I don't want your schoolwork to suffer."

The teenager rushed forward and enveloped Avery in a tight hug. "Thanks for taking a chance on me. I won't let you down."

As she held Jess, Avery reminded herself she wasn't to become attached to Reed or Jess. Unfortunately it was too late for both.

Chapter Nine

That night after dinner as Jess and Reed sat side by side at her father's desk working on the shelter website, she said, "I brought up your idea of me doing a blog with Avery today after she read my paper, which she loved. She's putting it online tomorrow as my first entry."

"I told you that paper was great." Reed had been pleased when she asked him to proofread her assignment. "With your writing skills and the way you talked about the shelter, I could see you having a future in marketing. That is, if you don't choose a career in the computer field."

Since they'd started working on the shelter's website and the social-media plan, Jess had talked more than the entire time he'd been in Colorado before that. She'd started asking his opinion about issues with friends and her schoolwork. They'd talked about colleges and things that would help on her applications. When he told her what he thought, he saw glimpses of respect in her eyes. Hell, even the damned dog had softened toward him, growling at him only every other time he came near the mutt.

"Avery said my volunteering at the shelter and doing stuff like the blog will look good on college applications. I'm thinking about volunteering there even after I'm done with the community-service gig."

While he looked forward to working with Jess on shelter business after dinner each night, he wasn't keen on how many of her sentences started with the words *Avery said.*

"You've been a big help with the website, Jess. You've got a real talent for web design."

"Another compliment? From you? I can't believe it."

He stared at his niece. Had he been that quick to criticize, but slow to praise? Yet another legacy from his father that he needed to overcome.

Still beaming from his praise, Jess said, "When are we going to show Avery what we've come up with?"

"If we get these last tweaks done tonight, you can show her tomorrow."

"You'll come with me to present it, right?"

"We'll do a dry run of the presentation to prepare you, but it's probably best you leave my name out of it. If Avery knows I helped with the design she'll probably hate it on principle."

"If a guy went to all this work for me, I'd think it was sweet. I bet Avery would, too. You should tell her. I know you like her."

That hardly described what he felt for Avery. Obsessed about. Craved. Needed, almost to the point that he couldn't sleep at night. Those sentiments came much closer.

"Giving her suggestions about her job and running the shelter was what got me into trouble. Promise you won't mention my name when you talk to Avery."

"I think you're wrong, but I promise."

AVERY GLANCED UP from the paperwork spread across her desk and smiled at Jess standing in the doorway.

"Can I talk to you for a minute, if you're not too busy?" the teenager asked, a nervous smile quivering on her lips.

"I've always got time for you."

As Avery said the words, she realized they weren't simply a nicety she tossed out. She truly meant them. Since Jess had started volunteering at the shelter, they'd come to know each other, and she caught glimpses of herself in the teenager.

Jess possessed a good heart and a gentle soul under all the harsh makeup. She took the world's problems, or at least the shelter's, to heart. *Just like I did at her age.*

"I was looking at the shelter's website and it got me thinking. I took a class on web design last summer." After she sank into the chair opposite Avery, Jess reached into her backpack, pulled out her computer and placed it on her lap. Her gaze remained riveted on her hands resting on the laptop. "I've been thinking about the shelter's website a lot lately. I started playing with some ideas, and I put together a new website for you to look at."

"I'd love to see it." Avery moved a stack of papers from her desk to the one open spot on the credenza behind her. "Scoot your chair over here, and show me."

A big smile on her face, Jess placed her computer on the desk in front of Avery and turned it on. While the machine booted up, the teenager moved her chair beside Avery's.

"I can't believe you created a website in your free time. Designing one is a lot of work."

"That's what people think, but it's not that big a deal when you know what you're doing."

When the website appeared on the screen, Avery leaned forward in her chair. "Wow. I don't know what to say. This is incredible! It's so professional."

The soft peach tones were a vast improvement over the dark colors they currently had. Below the shelter's logo were the page buttons. Beneath that, a banner contained an idyllic picture of a family gazing lovingly at the family dog. The animal snuggled up against the young son and daughter. Beside the photo on the left was the phrase "Celebrating pets and the people who love them." To the right were adoption and donation icons.

Jess scrolled down the site. "Stuff like the Pennies for Paws and the Pet Walk were scattered all over the page before. Putting them all here makes it easier for users to find what they need." She pointed to the left side of the screen. "All they have to do is scroll down."

"I agree. I can't wait to show this to the board. And you did this all on your own? You've got some skills, girl."

Beside her, Jess tensed ever so slightly. "I'm glad you like it."

The words were right, but Jess's tone was wrong. What had happened? Avery thought about what she'd said. "Are you worried about me taking this to the board for approval?"

"Not too much."

If it wasn't the board, then what had caused the change? *And you did this all on your own?*

Reed had been a computer whiz. In high school he and his dad had fought over him wanting to computerize the ranch's finances and breeding records. His father had insisted he didn't need a "damned machine" to do the brain work for him. Now Reed owned a large computer semiconductor company. Avery pegged him as the kind of owner who kept a close eye on every aspect of his business, including the company's website.

Jess is worried I'll be mad if I find out Reed helped her.

But that didn't make sense. Mr. Workaholic wouldn't take time away from his business to revamp the shelter website. She was imagining things.

"Do you want to present this to the board?"

Jess shook her head. "Ms. Stinson will have a cow if she finds out I was the one who created this."

"Come on. Seeing that would be worth it right there."

Jess giggled. "Definitely, but it's more important that the shelter gets a good website. Hopefully the new site will help with the fund-raising."

The tightness in Avery's chest loosened. She'd been right with her first instincts. Jess was worried the board would reject the design if they knew a teenager had created it. Reed had had nothing to do with this.

Good thing, because if he had, she might have to rethink the whole he-was-a-complete-ass thing.

WHEN JESS TOLD REED she needed a dress for the Fall Social, his first instinct was to give her his credit card. Then common sense kicked in. Giving a teenage girl his credit card, even with a strict spending limit, sounded as smart as asking a coyote to watch Thor. But that wasn't his biggest worry. After seeing Jess's fashion choices, his worst nightmare was that she'd come back with a skintight dress made out of cellophane wrap.

While he hadn't wanted the guardian role, he'd taken it on and he wasn't about to slough it off. He could handle shopping with Jess now that their relationship had improved. He was a man who knew what looked good on a woman. That didn't mean he'd enjoy the task. In fact, sitting in the dad/husband chair in a small women's boutique waiting while Jess tried on dresses felt as if he'd died and gone to hell.

After ten minutes, she strolled out of the dressing room, a scrap of red fabric tossed over her arm. "This one's perfect."

"What? I sat here all this time, and I don't get to see it on you?"

"I told you it's great. Don't you trust me?"

He bit his tongue to keep from blurting out hell no, she was a teenager. "My footing the bill entitles me to see the dress on you."

"Like you know what's fashionable."

"I live in California, and I date a lot."

He thought about his previous relationships. Whenever a woman hinted about getting serious, he moved on. He stopped calling, ignored her texts and let her calls go to voice mail. If she failed to get the hint, he tossed out his standard excuse that work had gotten demanding. Then he'd suggest they take a break, and that ended things.

Remembering his anger-management class, he focused on his breathing, counted to ten and then replied in a calm voice, "If I don't see the dress on you, I don't buy it. That's the deal."

She stood there glaring at him. "Are you serious?"

"Absolutely."

She whirled around and stormed back into the dressing room, only to emerge a minute later.

His jaw dropped, and for a moment he had no idea what to say other than she looked as if she belonged in a singles bar or on an episode of *Jersey Shore.*

How did she get the skintight red thing on? Nonstick

cooking spray had to be involved. He bit his tongue and counted to ten. While he might not know what was suitable for a fourteen-year-old girl, he sure knew what wasn't when he saw it. "Keep looking. That one's a no. It's not appropriate."

So much for their improved relationship. The teenage defiance he'd become so familiar with returned to her gaze full force. This was not going the way he imagined. Okay, maybe his idea that she'd try on a couple of dresses and buy something modest and longer hadn't been realistic, but this was insane.

"There's nothing wrong with it. *Everyone's* wearing dresses like this."

Right. Every twentysomething *woman* who was out trolling for a man. He doubted any parent of a teenage girl would let her out of the house in the dress. "Maybe so, but I know when a woman looks desperate for attention, and that dress screams it."

Pain filled Jess's eyes. Reed cringed. How could he be such an ass? He was his father's son. That was how. The man had never cared who he crushed as long as he won the argument.

Why the hell do you want to study business? You think you can be one of those big-shot CEOs? Not hardly. You were raised on a ranch. You might leave, but you'll never get the smell of manure out of your nose.

His mind raced, trying to figure out a way to salvage the situation. His confidence faded. He was out of his league. When he encountered resistance in business he stated the facts, relied on research and pointed out past trends. But this? He had nothing. No experience. No facts, and he knew squat about teenage fashion trends.

"I don't need you to pay for it. Dad gave me a credit card to use for emergencies."

"Good try, but no."

"I knew I should've asked Avery to go shopping with me. I never should've told you about the dance." Jess stormed back into the dressing room.

Reed sat there, his fingers digging into the upholstered arms of the chair, clueless as to what to do. He needed help. Avery would've done a much better job.

That's what he needed. An expert. At least Avery had once been a fourteen-year-old girl. She couldn't be as clueless as he was. He grabbed his cell phone and dialed. When Avery answered he blurted out, "Don't hang up. I need to talk to you about Jess."

"Is she okay?" Concern laced Avery's voice.

He explained the situation, and how things had disintegrated. "The dress Jess wants to buy looks like it belongs on a twenty-five-year-old who's out to hook a husband the old-fashioned way. Come convince her that I'm right and she needs to pick out a more appropriate dress."

"I can't. I'm on my way to John Sampson's to examine his new foal."

"That's perfect. Stop by the store on your way to his place. It'll take five minutes, tops. You'll come in, tell Jess the dress is awful and then you're done." When Avery didn't jump at his suggestion, he added, "All I've done so far is make her mad. Help me out here. Please?"

Her sigh radiated over the phone lines. "I'm not doing this for you. I'm doing it for Jess, so she doesn't get made fun of at the dance."

He didn't care why Avery agreed, as long as she did.

As Avery drove across town she imagined Reed's response if he thought Jess's choice inappropriate. Reed, always strong-minded and sure of himself. He'd probably made things worse with some stupid comment like the one he'd made to her on the phone about the dress being one a woman would wear to "hook a husband the old-fashioned way." Everything Jess did lately screamed of her need for attention, but he couldn't seem to understand that. Instead his responses fueled the teenager's natural inclination to prove she knew better.

They were two stubborn mules who'd die of starvation rather than share the feed trough.

When Avery walked into the small boutique she found Reed sulking in a chair, Jess's red backpack at his feet. He nodded toward the dressing rooms. "She's in there."

Avery grabbed a shirt off the closest rack and headed inside. "Jess?"

The teenager poked her head out from behind a red curtain in the middle room. "What are you doing here?"

"I stopped in to do a little shopping. When I went to try on this top, I saw your uncle outside the dressing room. I hear you're looking for a dress for the dance. Have you found one?"

"I did, but Uncle Stick-in-the-Mud says he won't pay for it." Jess reached behind her, grabbed the garment and showed the dress to Avery. Then she bit her lip and her eyes teared up. "He said it makes me look like I'm desperate for attention."

Yup. The situation had played out pretty much as she'd expected. "Like he knows about women's fashion. Try the dress on and let me see. Maybe we can work on him together and change his mind."

"You'd do that?"

"We women have to stick together against the chauvinistic, arrogant men of the world." Avery pulled back the curtain on the dressing room next to Jess's and placed the shirt on the hook inside while Jess smiled and ducked back into her room. A minute later she waltzed out. On top of being bright red and skintight, the thing was short enough that Avery wouldn't have had the nerve to wear it. After plastering a smile on her face, she motioned for Jess to follow her.

When they met Reed, Avery knew immediately what he wanted—for her to blast Jess with how tacky she looked and tell her to find something else. Didn't he realize that tactic wouldn't work any better for her than it had for him?

As Jess preened in front of the three-way mirror, Avery pretended to critically study the dress from all angles. "That dress is so cute." She forced out the words, thankful when she didn't choke on them.

Then she caught Reed's expression in the mirror. His eyes bulged at her words and he looked as if he'd jump out of his chair any minute. The man had the patience of a four-month-old puppy. She was willing to back him up, mainly because he was right about the dress, but not in the approach he expected. Her way would get the job done while smoothing Jess's ruffled feathers, but it would take time. Her gaze locked with his and she smiled, hoping to calm his rising temper.

"I'm not sure about the color, though." Avery paused. Finesse. That's what the situation required. "Have I ever told you how much I learned about fashion, especially what colors look good on people, when my sister-in-law shot Rory's commercial at the ranch?"

"That's right. Your brother's a model," Jess said, her gaze softening.

"Elizabeth spent a lot of time picking out the shirt he wore for the commercial. She had to make sure the color was right for him."

The teenager smoothed her hand over the red dress, uncertainty flashing in her eyes. "What's wrong with the color?"

"You've got such a great complexion, perfect really, but the color of the dress has an orange cast. It makes your skin look a little yellow."

The teenager stared at her reflection. "Really?"

Avery turned to Reed. "You see what I mean, don't you, Reed? This dress does nothing for her beautiful coloring."

He nodded obediently. "You're right. I don't know how I missed it."

"Guys never notice subtleties. They just know a dress isn't right, but they don't know why." Avery glanced at Reed and shook her head. "We can find something that has the good features of this dress, but in a color that suits you better."

As she and Jess walked through the shop, Avery steered Jess to more appropriate dresses. She picked up a couple of garments, mumbling comments about them being too young for such a mature teenager and then replaced them. Biting her lip, she selected a pink dress with a high round neck and a blousy fit, and pointed to Reed. "I bet this is something he'd think you should wear."

"What's wrong with it? I think it's cute," Reed responded, a glare darkening his features.

She and Jess giggled. Over the teenager's head, she noticed Reed smiling. Maybe he'd caught on to the game after all.

Next Avery selected a dress with a simple black tank-style top and a flowing skirt with a bold tie-dyed print. "This would be fantastic on you. It would highlight your great skin and make your eyes sparkle."

"It looks awfully long," Jess commented.

"We can hem it. That's no big deal if the rest of the dress works." She held the dress up to the teenager. "I have the perfect necklace to go with this. One with Swarovski crystals that I could lend you."

Five minutes later, Jess returned to the dressing room to try on four completely appropriate dresses.

"How about that? The big bad businessman had to call in reinforcements to deal with a teenage girl," Avery taunted as she stood beside Reed. "You can't always lay down the law with her. It only makes her dig in her heels and want to get the best of you. She's strong-willed and knows her own mind. Kind of like someone else I know." That was a big part of Reed and Jess's problem. They were too alike. "Sometimes all banging your head against a brick wall gets you is a major headache."

"I'm smart enough to know when to call in an expert in the field to avoid a bloody battle."

"For a moment when we first came out of the dressing room, I thought you were going to blow everything."

"When I heard you say that damned dress was cute, I almost did, but then I realized what you were up to."

Before he could respond, Jess returned, looking like a beautiful young woman. Avery smiled. "Jess, you look gorgeous. Doesn't she look amazing, Reed?"

"She looks beautiful." Jess beamed at her uncle's genuine praise.

"Do you have some heels that would go with this dress?" Jess shook her head, and Avery asked what size shoe she wore. "I wear a half size bigger, but I might have something you could borrow."

"And you'll loan me that great jewelry you told me

about?" Avery nodded, and Jess stared into the mirror. "You're sure we can get this hemmed in time?"

"Absolutely. Have your uncle drop you off at my house tonight. We'll pin up your dress and you can raid my closet for shoes." She'd also drop some subtle hints about makeup.

"What time? If you like pizza we could bring dinner."

"That's the least I can do," Reed added. "Is pizza with spinach and fresh tomatoes from McCabe's still your favorite?"

He remembered what kind of pizza she liked? So what if he did? He'd been an ass at the shelter the other day. Bringing her pizza wouldn't fix that.

Snarky words about what he could do with that idea sat perched on her tongue. Then she caught the look of excitement and anticipation shining in Jess's eyes. Eating pizza and hemming her dress were the kind of things she'd done with her mother before big high-school dances. "I'll see you at Twin Creeks around six."

"You're still living at home with your mom?" Reed asked.

"For now."

After Jess skipped off to the dressing room, Reed said, "The way you managed her was pretty damned amazing."

"Since my work here is done, I'm off to the Sampson place."

When she turned to leave, he reached out and placed a hand on her arm. "I know I'm bringing pizza tonight, but let me buy you a nice dinner Friday to thank you for saving my ass. I'll pick you up after I take Jess to the dance. She was about to deck me when I called you."

Her regret kicked in as she pulled away from him.

"I agreed to you bringing pizza for Jess's sake and to keep from making a scene, but as far as I'm concerned you're just somebody that I used to know."

"Let me make it up to you Friday."

"You aren't getting this. I don't like who you are now, but even if I did, I'm busy Friday night. My friend's the guidance counselor at the high school, and when they were coming up short on chaperones, she called in a favor. I'll be at the dance Friday night playing chaperone."

"Mrs. Palmer said we still need volunteers, Uncle Reed," Jess said as she strolled out of the dressing room, her selection clutched in her hand. "I told her I'd ask you to help out."

"I'd be happy to."

Avery flinched as he flashed her an I've-got-you-now grin.

If that's what he thought, he was so wrong. "We've already done the high-school dance thing. Remember? I don't know about you, but I have no desire to relive those years."

Chapter Ten

"Call me when I need to pick you up," Reed said to Jess as he pulled up in front of the sprawling ranch house at Twin Creeks.

"You're not coming in?"

Avery had made it quite clear this afternoon that he wasn't welcome. A disturbing sense of loss filled him. When he and Avery had dated, they'd studied at her house after he finished his chores, which often turned into him staying for dinner. Twin Creeks had given him a glimpse into what normal family life could be. "I've got work to do."

"Sure you do. It doesn't have anything to do with the fact that Avery's still mad. If you'd tell her about the website, she wouldn't be, you know."

The McAlister house had been the closest thing to a home he'd ever really had, and now he was unwelcome because of the person who'd once gained him entrance.

Avery. She made him laugh. She kept him on his toes and made him think about the world outside his office. And she lit a fire in him, a need so deep that it left him wanting to be the kind of man she respected.

But what could he offer her? Sure, he could offer her financial stability, but what else? Certainly not children.

Dealing with Jess was one thing. Children of his own? He refused to tempt fate.

He turned to Jess. "I don't want Avery knowing about the website."

She jerked the truck door open and stomped up the walkway to the front door, carrying the pizza box to Nannette McAlister, who greeted her on the porch.

As the pair exchanged words, he waved. Mrs. McAlister didn't wave back, but instead strode toward the truck, her brow furrowed. He rolled down the passenger window and braced himself for a lecture.

"It's bad enough that I heard about you coming home from Mabel Withers. With as many meals as you had at this house I deserved better than that, and now I hear you're not staying tonight."

Instead of making him feel guilty, her concern pleased him. He knew the more she picked at him, the more she cared. "Mrs. McAlister, you're looking as pretty as ever."

While heavier than she'd been years ago, she still looked very much like the woman he remembered. Her short spiky hair, now flecked with silver, added to her saucy look.

"Flattery won't get you out of hot water with me, Reed Montgomery, but you just keep on trying."

"I'd have to be a fool to think a compliment would do that, Mrs. McAlister. I'd love to stay for dinner, but I have work to do."

"What are you going to do? Go home and make dinner for yourself? Or skip eating?" Hands on her hips, she continued, "The work will still be there later, and don't you think it's about time you started calling me Nannette?"

Knowing the futility of arguing with her when she

had her mind set, he turned off the ignition and climbed out of the truck.

When he joined her on the walkway, she enveloped him in a hug like the ones he'd once received from his mother. "It's good to see you, son. You've been gone too long."

"You may not say that after tonight. When we saw Avery today, she was still pretty mad at me."

Jess stared at him as if he had the intelligence of a two-year-old when they joined her on the porch. "If you'd tell her about—"

"The longer we stand here, the colder the pizza gets." He tossed his niece a keep-quiet glare.

Nannette glanced between him and Jess, her confused stare lingering on him, indicating she figured something was up, but instead of saying anything, she opened the front door and stepped aside for them to enter.

As Avery's mother led them through the house to the kitchen, she said, "Avery told me all about the dance and your dress, Jess. I can't wait to see it on you."

The ease he'd felt when he walked into the McAlister house disappeared when he walked past the room that had been Ben McAlister's study. Reed's stomach twisted.

Nannette's and Jess's voices created a buzz around him. He forced himself to keep walking as the memories clawed at him, threatening to pull him under.

He still remembered sitting in that office, scared to death about going to jail and disgusted with how he'd lost control and beaten his father until the man begged for mercy. He still remembered what Avery's father had said that night.

All you'll do is drag my daughter down with you.

A hand touched his arm. Nannette was staring at him, worry etched on her face. "Are you all right, dear?"

Words refused to form in his head.

Nannette squeezed his arm. "Let it go. It's time."

"I don't know how."

"Reed, I'll give you a bit of wisdom like I would my own children." Nannette's eyes filled with the same loving look he remembered from his own mother, and his heart ached over what he'd lost. "We can choose to remember the past, or we can put it in its place and look to the future."

Jess glanced over her shoulder. "What's going on? Is something wrong?"

Shoving his memories back into the dark cavern of his mind, he smiled at his niece and walked toward her. "Nothing's wrong. Let's eat."

When they walked into the kitchen Avery frowned. "I didn't expect you to come tonight." Then she turned her back and opened the kitchen cupboard.

Message received. He should've dropped Jess and the pizza off.

"I should leave."

Nannette glanced between him and her daughter. "Absolutely not. I invited you to dinner and you accepted. Whatever's going on between the two of you is just that, between you two. Now, let's all sit down at the table."

Awkward silence enveloped the McAlister kitchen, periodically broken by the clunk of glasses on the wooden table.

"Has Jess told you what a great help she's been at the shelter?" Nannette finally said.

"Baxter almost escaped today on his walk with Mrs. Hartman." Jess opened the pizza box and grabbed another slice, having devoured her first one with unlady-like speed. "I think he's tired of being at the shelter."

"So I'm not the only one who can't control him?" Reed froze. The minute he'd spoken the words, he regretted them. Avery's eyes darkened. Her lips pressed into a thin colorless line.

Why the hell hadn't he kept his mouth shut? Why did he bait her?

Because even her irritation was better than indifference. Love and hate. Two sides of the same coin. As long as she got angry, she still cared.

"I bet Mrs. Hartman wasn't distracted because she was on the phone." Avery stared at him, challenging him to deny her statement.

"The nasty looks flying between the two of you are bad enough. Poor Jess and I feel like we're in a combat zone. I won't tolerate snide comments. If you don't start being nice to each other, I may just lock you in a room together and refuse to let you out until you solve your problems."

Reed laughed, but noticed Avery didn't share his humor.

"She means it." Avery shuddered. "She did that once to Rory and Griffin. They were in there for an hour."

"That's a great idea, Mrs. McAlister," Jess said. "I say we do it."

"Truce?" Reed asked.

Avery nodded.

"How's the fund-raising going?" Reed asked, hoping to steer the conversation to a safer topic.

"I asked the exec Griffin put me in touch with to donate five thousand dollars, thinking I'd be happy if they donated half that, and he agreed."

Reed smiled. "I see you took my advice."

"For your information, I was already doing what you suggested."

"Both of you know my rules about the dinner table." Nannette's calm, flat voice echoed through the room.

"Yes, ma'am," she and Reed replied in unison.

Those who fought at the table went away hungry. "Either get along or leave."

"I've got a better idea," Avery said as she stood. "Jess, if you're done eating, we should get to work on your dress." Then she scooted out of the kitchen before he could object.

THE NEXT NIGHT AVERY STOOD with her friend Rachel, the school's counselor, in their old high-school gym, decorated with purple, white and silver streamers. "Remind me again what this chaperone gig entails," she said, taking a sip of watery fruit punch from the plastic glass she clutched in her hand.

"It's pretty simple. We make sure none of the kids sneak off, spike the punch or do anything else inappropriate," Rachel said. "With you here, I can keep my eye on the troublemakers."

Since her statement opened the door, Avery figured she might as well walk through it and see what she could learn about Jess. "Is Jess Montgomery part of that group?"

"No. I couldn't believe it when I heard about what happened with the shelter. She's going through a tough time, but I suspect she got pulled into something. She's so afraid of losing her friends. That's her biggest problem."

"That's what I thought, too."

She scanned the gym as a dutiful chaperone should, and spotted Reed and Jess as they entered. While Jess headed for a group of girls clustered under one of the basketball hoops, Reed stood inside the door, looking as sexy as ever in black jeans and T-shirt paired with a black blazer. A tan Stetson and boots completed his look.

"Is that Jess's uncle? Mr. Tall, Dark and Dreamy who just walked in?"

Avery nodded.

"That man looks fine." Rachel practically drooled as she watched Reed walk toward them. "I've heard you two were once an item. Have you picked back up where you left off, or is he fair game?"

What was it with her friends? Emma had asked if Avery minded if she made a play for Reed, and now Rachel. *You'd think he was the only eligible bachelor in town.*

"I don't care who Reed dates."

Better duck for cover before God sends a lightning bolt to strike you down for that monster lie.

When Reed joined them, Rachel morphed into someone else before Avery's eyes. Her confident friend who possessed a master's degree in counseling and had graduated magna cum laude from Duke twirled a strand of auburn hair around her finger, smiled and peered up at Reed.

"Thank you for agreeing to chaperone the dance. We don't get many fathers volunteering, much less uncles."

"No problem." Reed turned to Avery, his gaze unreadable. "Thanks again for your help with Jess. She looks great *and* appropriate."

"I was happy to help her." Avery's throat tightened. This stilted conversation was worse than arguing with him.

Rachel flirted with Reed, tossing her hair and giggling at his jokes. Her friend had been working with teenagers too long, Avery thought, because tonight she was acting like one. After five minutes, Avery excused herself, claiming she needed to go to the restroom.

It was going to be a long night.

Once in the bathroom, she splashed cold water on her face. She needed to get a grip. She kept telling herself she wasn't interested in Reed, and yet whenever another woman showed interest, her nose got out of joint.

Figure out what you want, and either fish or cut bait.

Resisting the urge to hide in the bathroom to avoid the issue altogether, she squared her shoulders and headed back to the gym.

Untwist your big-girl panties and deal with it.

When she returned, she spotted Jess at the punch bowl and joined her to say hello. "You look amazing, Jess."

"Thanks." The teenager fingered the crystal-and-rose-quartz necklace that Avery had loaned her. "I just saw a couple sneak off to the janitor's closet."

Avery searched for Rachel, but couldn't locate her. The she noticed Reed was nowhere to be found, either. Surely they couldn't have gone somewhere together. She almost laughed. Rachel was the school's counselor. No way would she go off with one of the chaperones. But then where were they? "I'll find Ms. Palmer. She'll know how to deal with this."

Jess shrugged. "Okay. It's not my problem if Haley and Brad have half their clothes off by the time she gets there. You two can explain it to their parents, the principal and the—"

"Where's the closet?"

Avery followed Jess through the halls. The last thing she needed was to be blamed for two teenagers going at it like rabbits while she was chaperoning the dance. Harper would rake her over the coals for that. She could hear her board president now. *How can we trust you to manage the shelter and its funds properly when you can't supervise a group of teenagers at a dance?*

When they reached the closet, Avery knocked on the door. "You're busted. Come out now."

"I'd love to, but the door's locked."

"Reed?" Avery turned to Jess. "What's going on?"

The teenager revealed a key ring, unlocked the door and shoved Avery inside with a surprising amount of force, sending her careening into Reed. Her momentum threw him off balance as he wrapped his strong arms around her.

Before they could regain their footing, the door slammed shut and the deafening sound of the lock clicking echoed in the small closet.

"Jess, unlock the damned door," Reed yelled as he banged on the door.

"Let us out," Avery pleaded.

"Not until you talk about why you're mad at each other."

"I promise we will. Just let us out." Avery's mind spun, trying to think of how to convince the teenager. "You can trust me, Jess, really. We'll work this out."

"I don't know. Mrs. McAlister told you to work things out last night, but you didn't."

"We will now. Won't we, Reed?" Avery turned toward the man fuming beside her. "Tell her!"

"What's important here is you're asking for trouble doing this." Reed's voice rippled with frustration.

Avery poked him in the ribs and whispered, "Don't say that."

"I don't know where you got the keys to this closet,

but that alone could get you into trouble," Reed continued.

"Now's not the time for a lecture." Avery ground out the words, trying to fill her voice with force, while remaining quiet enough that Jess couldn't hear. "Remember the dress-shop incident."

"It doesn't matter how I got the keys. What's important is I have them and I didn't steal them."

"If you don't let us out right now, you're grounded. I'm taking away your phone, your computer, the TV and anything else I can think of." Reed's voice rattled with the force of his anger.

"Then I might as well get my money's worth." The *tap, tap* of high heels on industrial tile faded.

"Why couldn't you keep your mouth shut? I almost had us out of here." Avery banged on the door. "You just *had* to play the hard-ass in charge."

Yup, he'd screwed up again. Despite the way he acted with Avery and Jess, he was a logical, rational, good guy. Why couldn't he do something right when Avery was around? Because all his blood got diverted from his brain the moment he saw her and his testosterone overrode his common sense.

He upended a crate of rags, sat it in front of Avery and patted it. "We might as well get comfortable, since it looks like we'll be here for a while." He turned over a second one and settled his long frame awkwardly on the makeshift chair. "We can't go on like this. We didn't always see things the same way, but we respected each other. Didn't we?"

"So what happened? What's going on between us now?"

"Beats the hell out of me." He stood, needing to

pace, but realized that he couldn't take more than a step or two.

"You asked me the other night if I wondered what things could be like between us now."

He nodded and held his breath, not sure where she was headed with the conversation and not liking the tightness in his chest.

"Since you asked me that, I've been wondering about it. A lot."

He'd sure as hell been thinking about the same thing, almost nonstop, but where had her thoughts led her? Probably not the same place as his—that they'd burn each other up from the heat they generated if they ever got together again.

How did a man respond to a comment like that? Certainly not with what he was thinking. Glancing at Avery, he tried to think of what to say, but decided his best bet was to keep his mouth shut.

In the dim light from the overhead bulb, he saw Avery swallow. Then she licked her lips. "What do you think of us becoming friends with benefits?"

Avery's words stopped Reed in his tracks. He collapsed onto the crate. He was dreaming. He'd fallen, hit his head and was suffering from a brain injury. He was hearing things. Any of those were more likely than that he'd actually heard Avery say they should start having casual sex.

"Excuse me?"

"We're both wondering about it. If we become—" She paused, shifting her weight. The plastic crate under her squeaked. "If we did get more involved, we'd know, and then we can both move on."

He frowned. Obviously she wasn't as excited by the thought as he was. Why would she think he'd settle for that? He wanted more from her. The revelation left him weak. "What do you mean 'move on'?"

"It's like when I tried to give up chocolate for Lent one time. Once I decided to do that, I saw chocolate everywhere I went. Someone brought brownies to work. Emma wanted a chocolate cake for her birthday. The more I tried to resist the cravings, the stronger they got." She folded her hands on her lap in an uncharacteristically demure pose. "After Lent was over and I could have all the chocolate I wanted, I found it wasn't a big deal."

What the hell was going on? Casual sex didn't fit with the Avery he knew. Then he really looked at her and noticed her picking at her nails. She did that only when she was nervous.

He stood, stumbled the two steps to close the distance between them and knelt in front of her. His hands covered hers. Then words he never thought he'd say if a gorgeous woman asked him to have no-strings-attached sex with her tumbled out of him. "Could we start with going on a date?"

Her crystal-blue eyes darkened like a stormy sea. She pulled her hands out from under his and crossed her arms over her chest. "You don't want me? You're telling me no?"

He'd have laughed at her ridiculous assumption, but he knew it would piss her off more. "That's not what I meant."

She scoffed. "Then explain it to me."

"If you and I make love again, it will be a very big deal, and it won't be just a casual fling." He linked his hands with hers and drew her to her feet. Then he lowered his lips to hers. Her body instantly relaxed and molded to his. Fire raced through him as if he were made of drought-stricken grass. Avery clung to him, her hands running over him, exploring, teasing, fueling his need.

He ran his hands through her hair, marveling at the silken texture. Her lips nibbled at the sensitive spot where his neck joined his shoulder as she ground her pelvis against his hard flesh. Blood pounded in his ears, blotting out every thought but the feel of her in his arms.

Her heated breath fanned his neck. He'd been missing out on so much by shutting himself off emotionally for years. "Avery, I've missed you. More than I ever realized."

"I'm right here. Where I've always been."

His mouth captured hers, all the longing he'd felt for years flowing out of him into her.

A click sounded somewhere around him, but he ignored the sound. A door creaked and giggles echoed in the small room. He and Avery jumped apart. He ran a hand through his disheveled hair, while Avery straightened her blouse. A few minutes longer and who knows what Jess would've walked in on.

"I knew you two liked each other, but, jeez, you're setting a bad example."

Jess had returned to release them. There was no denying the truth now.

THE NEXT MORNING AS AVERY examined the shelter's newest feline arrival she realized she and Reed had never actually decided how to proceed with their relationship. They'd talked about dating, but then they got distracted. She smiled at the memory of Reed's kisses.

After Jess discovered them in the closet, they'd spent the remainder of the night talking, dancing and being proper chaperones. When the dance ended he walked her to her car and kissed her good-night.

But where did they go from here?

"Emma said I'd find you here." Reed's strong voice sent excitement coursing through her system.

She looked up to find him leaning against the door-jamb of the exam room, none of the uncertainty or awkwardness that she felt over what happened last night evident on his classic features.

"Want to go out for dinner and a movie tonight?"

"Sure." She scratched the tabby behind his ears in effort to keep her hands from fidgeting. She hadn't been this nervous the first time he asked her out when they were both sixteen.

He smiled, and butterflies set up residence in her stomach, their wings beating at a frantic pace. "I'll pick you up at seven."

Then he said he knew she was busy and was gone before she could protest, leaving her just as unsure about where things stood between them. Guess she'd find out tonight.

She finished the cat's exam and turned him over to Carly—a part-time vet tech and a prime example of why never to judge a book by its cover. The tech might look tough with all her arm tattoos, piercings and short spiky ebony hair, but there wasn't a softer heart around.

She returned to her office to check her emails. One week. That's all they had left until the Pet Walk. They'd registered a record number of people for the event. At fifteen dollars each, they'd already exceeded last year's total in that regard. Many of the attendees had said they'd stepped up their pledging efforts, which would help, too. Smaller sponsors had kicked in twice as much money as last year, while Devlin Designs and Griffin's network had each donated five thousand dollars. Those amounts still floored her. In previous years, the shelter's largest sponsors gave, at most, two thousand dollars. Any other year she'd be thrilled with what they'd achieved, but would all her work be enough to reach their goal?

The first thing she noticed when she reached her office was the big black leather desk chair with a giant bow wrapped around it.

Even before she opened the card placed on the seat, she knew it had come from Reed. She lifted the envelope and sank onto the chair. Air whooshed out from under her. She leaned back and sighed. Now, *this* was a chair.

Inside the envelope she discovered a sheet of folded computer paper. Reed's bold handwriting was scrawled across the page. "Consider this an early Christmas gift. I didn't want you to have to wait for Santa. Enjoy. Reed."

That was so like the man she'd fallen in love with years ago. She'd wondered if the sensitive Reed was still there, buried deep within the workaholic. Now she knew.

But what should she do about her feelings? The things that drove them apart, his living in California, her life being in Colorado and their different expectations about children, still existed.

But things were different, too. Reed would be here for a year until Colt returned from Afghanistan. They had time to figure things out. Maybe his views on children would change after spending time with Jess. He probably didn't realize it, but his relationship with Jess had changed a lot already.

Nothing ventured, nothing gained. If she didn't explore a relationship with Reed now, she'd always wonder what might have been. Better knowing than forever wondering.

She wanted to see Reed to tell him how much she wanted to be with him.

History had repeated itself. She was in love with Reed. Again.

Chapter Eleven

Ten minutes later, Avery parked her truck by the Rocking M's barn, walked to Reed's front door and knocked. What could she say? *Hey, thanks for the desk chair. I don't think you're a complete ass anymore. In fact, I think I might be in love with you?*

Maybe not.

When he didn't answer, she walked to the barn. Once inside, she inhaled deeply, trying to control her racing thoughts. The familiar earthy smells washed over her. A horse nickered, and then she heard Reed's low voice.

"Hey, pretty lady. Let me take a look at that leg." The horse whinnied. "I'll be gentle."

His voice rippled through her, leaving her warmer than a man had in—well, she couldn't remember how long.

"That a girl. I need to figure out why you're favoring this leg." Mesmerized, she followed the sound of his voice.

Avery's heart fluttered. This was the Reed she used to know. The gentle cowboy who spent hours in the saddle with her exploring the world around them, who teased her and whom she loved to distraction.

She entered the stall and found him kneeling beside a chestnut mare, his large hands cradling the animal's hoof.

"Do you want me to take a look at her, since I'm here?"

"It's just a stone. I can handle it." He released the animal, reached into his back pocket and pulled out a pocketknife. "What are you doing here? You aren't going to cancel our date for tonight, are you?"

"I wanted to thank you in person for the chair."

"I thought I'd help Santa out this year." His boyish grin made her insides as gooey as caramel inside chocolate.

"It was very sweet of you. I'm sure it'll greatly increase my productivity."

"I'm glad you like it."

She thought about the website. Jess hadn't done the work by herself—Avery would bet on it. "You helped Jess with the website, didn't you?"

"Did she tell you? She promised me she wouldn't."

No matter what Jess said about designing a website being easy, doing one took time. Time that Reed had taken away from his own business to help hers. "She didn't say anything. I guessed. Why didn't you tell me?"

"You were pretty mad at me—not that I blame you." He worked to dislodge the stone. "I was an ass at the shelter, and you had every right to throw me out. I went on the shelter's website to make a donation, and then I realized you'd say I was taking the easy way out. I wanted to do something that would help you and the shelter, but Jess did all the hard work. I was just the idea man."

"I've known the website needed work, and the board's been on my case about it, but I didn't have the money or the time to deal with it." Avery stopped. This conversation wasn't going at all as she'd imagined, but then she wasn't sure what she'd expected.

You expected by now you'd be in his arms.

She'd made the move at the dance, and she wasn't about to do the same thing here. She possessed *some* pride. "I see the ranch work is coming back to you, city slicker."

"It's been like riding a horse, except for the sore muscles part."

"That's what you get for letting yourself go."

How had she gotten those words out, even as a joke?

He straightened, a mischievous glint in his eye. Then he leaned back on his heels. "Take a good long look, sweetheart. Then tell me you think I'm out of shape."

Her heart rate spiked. His jeans and tight T-shirt revealed a physique most men would sell their soul for. She could keep the shelter running for a year if she sold posters with a picture of him in this pose with the fire raging in his eyes like it was now. She'd seen that smoldering gaze countless of times before, but this was different. Reed was different. Stronger. Even more sure of himself and, she guessed, more sure of what he could make her feel.

As he advanced, the small confines of the horse stall became more intimate. The air crackled from the passion firing between them. His gaze raked over her. "Want me to prove what kind of shape I'm in and how much stamina I've got?"

"Yes, please."

Reed smiled, and her heart did cartwheels. "I'll do my best."

"I said that out loud? I didn't mean to."

"I'm so glad you did, darling."

As he closed the distance between them, she realized

how much she wanted this. How much she needed *him,* and not just physically. He'd changed, but deep inside, he was the same man she'd loved since kindergarten. Strong. Decisive. Sensual. He was part of so many of the memories she held dear: birthdays, prom, graduation, being accepted to college.

Their lives were intertwined.

As his lips covered hers, she melted against him. Desperate to touch him, she pulled his shirt from his jeans and slid her hand under the material, finding warm, firm skin. Strong muscles flexed under her palms, and his groan rippled through her. It wasn't enough. She tugged at his shirt, but her hands tangled in the garment. He gently swept her hands aside and finished the task.

She stepped back to admire him. His broad chest rose and fell with his rapid breathing. "I take it back. Every last word I said about you being out of shape."

Then she was in his arms again, and his lips found hers. She deepened their kiss, growing bolder. Her hands moved over him, exploring and teasing as she reacquainted herself with his body. She refused to worry about the future. Nothing mattered right now but Reed and being with him.

AVERY FILLED HIS SENSES as her hands roamed over his heated body. Over in her stall, the horse nickered. What was he thinking? "We're too old to make love in the barn."

"I can't wait."

He cupped her face in his hands and kissed her. All the passion he felt, all the emotions he kept so tightly reined in poured out of him. He hadn't realized it, but he'd been dreaming of this moment for years. "I've made so many mistakes with you. I want to do this right."

"Trust me. You are."

She caressed him through his jeans. He moaned, and for a moment he gave in to the pleasure of her touch. Pleasure built, threatening to consume him. His control fading, he scooped her into his arms and headed for the barn door.

As he walked outside, she alternated between kissing his neck and nibbling on it. Her hands caressed his chest, finding his sensitive nipples, sending his motor revving into a new gear. "Keep that up and I might drop you."

"I'm capable of walking."

He set her on her feet, and pulled her against him. He ground his erection against her pelvis as his hands covered her breasts, kneading the tender flesh. Her steamy breath fanned his heated skin. When she moaned, he almost exploded. He lifted her again, and this time practically ran to the house.

Once in his room, he placed Avery on the bed. Despite vowing to go slowly, to savor every minute with her, he couldn't. They frantically worked to undress each other. Urgency and need churned inside him, growing with her every touch as they tumbled back onto the bed.

Her hands and mouth everywhere on his body tested his control, making him feel like an untried youth. As he caressed her heated flesh, she writhed beneath him, and her nails dug into his shoulder.

"Now. Please," she urged.

He rolled away from her and searched in the nightstand for a small foil packet. Seconds later, he pulled her under him. As he eased into her, he bit his lip to keep from crying out. How could he ever have left her?

They moved together. Tension escalated inside him, building and straining. His hand slipped between them and he stroked her. Her gaze locked with his. The naked emotion in her eyes stunned him. He'd never connected with anyone the way he had with Avery. She always could see into his soul.

He drove deeper and her body tightened around him as she climaxed, sending him to his own fulfillment.

Afterward, as he cradled Avery in his arms, Reed found a sense of peace he hadn't known he craved. What he'd found with her—the completeness, the fulfillment—left him stunned and more than a bit shaken. He remembered how much he loved her. How she'd kept him grounded and made him feel that he could do anything.

She awakened a part of him he'd thought no longer existed. The part that longed to be connected to someone. The part that knew life would be better if he came home every night to someone who loved and understood him. If he came home to Avery.

What had he done?

"Why'd you break up with me in an email? Why wouldn't you return my calls?"

He closed his eyes as her soft questions evaporated his joy. Memories crowded in on him.

"Mom said you've been running for years. Was I one of the things you were running from?"

He stiffened beside her, reluctant to spoil the perfection they'd shared, but she had the right to know. She deserved the truth. He owed her that. He should've told her before they made love, because knowing who he really was and the stock he came from could have changed her opinion of him.

"I told you things were bad at home, and I hated being there, but I never told you how bad things were. My dad used to beat my mother, and when she died, he started in on me and Colt." The story poured out of him. The helplessness he'd felt at first over his father's constant criticism and unrealistic demands, and how he'd resented his mother for staying. Instead of taking her sons and leaving the first time her husband beat her, she rationalized his behavior. If she were a better wife he wouldn't hit her. If the boys would do what their father said, everything would be fine.

The words his father hurled at him one night hammered away at him. *What makes you think you've got what it takes to make it anywhere but here? You think you're smart, but all that book-learning can't change who you are. You think you're better than me? You aren't. Mark my words, you'll be back here someday with your tail tucked between your legs.*

"That night I nearly beat my father to death made me take a hard look at my life. Your dad said he saw glimpses of my father in me. Like I didn't realize that every time I looked in the mirror. But he was right. My anger was getting out of control."

Her hands cupped his face, forcing him to meet her unwavering gaze. "I never once worried you'd hurt me."

"I did. I was worried enough that I took anger-management classes while I was at Stanford, and things got better. But when I'm here, I'm scared I'll get pulled back under. Your mom was right. I have been running. From my past. From my fear. From you.

"When I got to Stanford I could start over. No one knew me. I left my past behind. I couldn't come back.

Then I thought about you, and how I couldn't see you living in California. I couldn't ask you to leave your family. And you wanted kids. You'll be a wonderful mother someday. I see it every time you're with Jess. You always know how to handle things, how to make her feel better."

"You're doing better with her than you think."

He twined his fingers with hers, needing her strength, her comfort. "I've screwed up so many times with her it scares me."

"But you admit your mistakes and you work to fix them. That's what a good parent does."

"I couldn't deal with the stress." Avery, forever the optimist who saw the good in everyone, no matter how hard she had to look. "I wrote you an email and didn't return your calls because I couldn't bear anything more personal. I couldn't tell you how worried I was about dragging you down with me."

Her hand, the one not clutching his, rested on his chest above his heart. He wondered if she noticed how fast it was beating. "You should have told me. I'd have understood. I would've helped you."

Of course she would have. That was part of the problem, back then and now. She always knew what to do. She always cared. She was always too good for him.

Knowing he wasn't good enough for her, that he never would be, he gathered her into his arms. While the first time they made love had been unbelievable, they'd both been almost frantic. Now he wanted to take his time. He wanted to forget about everything else and lose himself in Avery.

THE DAY OF THE PET WALK, Avery arrived at Stanley Park at the unholy hour of six-thirty to begin setting up. Sun glistened off the mountains surrounding the park. She still couldn't believe how wonderful the past week had been. After she and Reed had made love that afternoon, she'd returned to the office and worked on details for the Pet Walk. Then she met Reed for dinner and a movie. Their first date. No doubt about it, she was madly in love with him. Since then, they had spent every spare hour in each other's company. And now she finally understood what had driven him away.

Her mom had been right. He'd been running from his father and his past. No wonder he hadn't wanted to return to Estes Park. Why couldn't he see what strength it took for him to be here?

But what about her? When she thought of her childhood, Reed was there in almost every memory. She suspected the same was true for him. Did that mean being with her dredged up things he'd rather keep buried? And if it did, could they ever move past that?

She refused to think about that.

Just enjoy being with him, and worry about the future later. You've got time. At least a year.

"You look like you could use some caffeine."

She turned to find Reed beside her, a white Starbucks cup in his hands and an endearing grin on his face.

"Tell me that's a nonfat vanilla latte."

He nodded, handed her the cup and kissed her cheek. "Some things about you never change."

She sipped her drink and felt the warmth seep into her. Heat from the coffee and from Reed's fervent gaze.

"I needed that." She glanced around. "Where's Jess?"

"I dropped her and Thor at the shelter. She's helping Carly with the animals she's bringing. What can I do? Consider me your executive assistant."

"Cool." She grinned wickedly at him. "My own personal assistant."

"Not that personal. At least, not here."

"Later?"

"Absolutely." He kissed her lightly, and electricity dashed through her from his tender touch. "What happens at one of these things?"

Avery pointed to the trail near the dog park. "Our vendors and sponsors set up tables along here. It's kind of like a mini pet mall. We've got pet products, rescue groups and local businesses. We've even got an airbrush artist this year who will paint a picture of someone's pet on a T-shirt or a hat. The best part is, he's donating a portion of his sales today." She pointed to the large shelter. "We'll have brats, chips and drinks for sale there. We've got a lot of people who are walking for pledges today, and they'll follow the trail."

"This is quite a production. I had no idea the event was this big. I'm impressed."

His genuine praise flowed over her.

"Avery?" Emma's voice came over the walkie-talkie in her pocket. "Grant Timmons wants to know if you picked up the podium from the church."

"It's in the back of my truck." She turned to Reed. "Since you have so wonderfully demonstrated what great shape you're in this week, would you mind providing a little extra muscle?" When he nodded, she spoke into the walkie-talkie. "I'm sending Reed to the parking lot. He'll help Grant unload the podium and get it in place."

While Reed saw to that task, Avery checked in with Carly to see what adoptable animals she'd brought to the event. She found her and a group of volunteers clustered around the shelter van unloading dogs. Hopefully a few of these souls would find forever homes today.

"How many dogs did you bring?"

"I've got seven. I'll go back for the cats. I thought I'd bring ten for the cat corner we'll set up in the small shelter."

Feeling Carly had things under control, Avery had turned to leave when she heard a particular bark. No. It couldn't be. Carly wouldn't. But as Avery stood there watching, Carly opened a crate and out jumped Baxter.

"Carly, can I speak with you for a second?" She pointed to a spot ten feet away under a group of trees.

"You brought Baxter? Carly, what were you thinking?"

"I was thinking this is his best shot to find a home." The dog strained against the leash the vet tech held. "Baxter, sit."

The dog barked and tugged harder.

"Baxter, sit," Avery said in her authoritative veterinarian voice. Instead of obeying, the dog jumped up on her. "Down." This time when he failed to listen, she stepped away, out of leash range. "We've never had a dog fight or an animal running loose before. I don't want to start today. Not when we've got so much at stake, and somehow Baxter always brings chaos with him."

Kind of like someone else she knew, though Reed appeared to be on his best behavior today.

"We've got to give Baxter this chance. I'll put a harness on him and have Nikki take him. She can handle him," Carly said, referring to one of their most experienced volunteers. Then she scratched Baxter's head. "How can you say no to this face? He deserves a shot to find his forever home."

How could she refuse that pitch? "I'll trust your judgment, but at the first sign of trouble, he's gone." Avery glared at the dog. "Got that, buddy? You don't get three strikes today. One and you're out. Don't blow this chance."

For the next hour Avery spoke with various vendors and sponsors as they set up their displays along the walkway. As she stood chatting with one of their biggest donors, the owner of the area pet cemetery, her phone rang. After mumbling a quick apology, she tugged it out of her pocket and glanced at the screen. Principal Jacobson. The high-school principal was scheduled to be one of the contest judges. When she answered, she discovered he'd eaten some bad sushi and wasn't going to be able to make it. She assured him it was fine and told him she hoped he felt better soon.

"One of your judges can't come?" Reed asked as she shoved her phone into her pocket.

"We'll be fine. I still have two judges." Harper and her teenage niece. Great. That meant Harper would be running the show. Avery chided herself for being so negative. Harper would be fine. She just didn't seem to get that these contests weren't really about who was "best," but about who showed the most heart. Last year's pet-lookalike winner had been a six-year-old girl with long curly brown hair and her white miniature poodle. When she was asked how she and her dog looked alike, she responded, "We're both beautiful inside and out," winning over the audience and the judges.

"I can fill in."

Reed's offer caught her off guard, but she was happy to take any help she could get.

"That would be great," she said, and proceeded to

fill him in on his duties, emphasizing that the events were meant to be fun and lighthearted.

With Reed at her side, she touched base with the remaining business people and sponsors. An important part of her duties included making sure everyone felt appreciated for their support and participation in the event, no matter how small.

"I get it now," Reed said after they spoke with an insurance agent. "You're really like a CEO."

She nodded. "Just on a smaller, more personal scale. But that's not why I went to vet school. When the shelter's doing well enough, I'll be glad to hire someone to take over my director duties."

"You don't enjoy that part of your job?"

She explained that when she'd taken the position, the plan had been that the shelter would hire a part-time director within six months. "I love being associated with the shelter and helping animals that don't have anyone. I love working with people, but I want to do more education, more working with pet owners. A lot of what I do now is management-related, writing grants and budgeting. Not exactly my thing."

A few feet in front of her, Avery spotted a familiar face and smiled. "Mrs. Russell, how are you today?"

"I'm still here, so I must be doing fairly well." Then the woman turned to Reed. "Do you remember me, young man?"

Avery stiffened. Reed had taken a class with Mrs. Russell in junior high, but would he remember the woman after all these years? "Reed's been gone a long time, Mrs. Russell, but I'm sure—"

"How could I forget you? I think of you every time I make pizza. I still use the recipe I got in your class."

The eighty-year-old blushed like a schoolgirl and pat-

ted Reed's hand. "I can admit it now that I'm retired—
you were one of my favorite students. You didn't think
cooking was beneath you, and you were always willing
to help other students who were culinarily challenged."

"That's kind of you to say, ma'am."

"I'm proud of you both," Mrs. Russell continued.
"Avery, you're doing wonderful work at the shelter, and,
Reed, I hear you've made quite a name for yourself in
the business world."

Not wanting that part of his life to intrude today,
Avery asked, "Are you entering Chandra in the best-
dressed pet contest?"

"Of course, dear. She's got to defend her title."

Reed grinned and raised his hand. "I've got to stop
you right there. As one of the judges, I shouldn't be
hearing this. I take my responsibilities very seriously."

"We wouldn't want anyone saying Chandra had an
unfair advantage because a judge heard that she's won
the contest the last three years in a row," Mrs. Russell
stated, her tone and expression serious.

"Exactly," Reed responded.

Avery checked her watch. "It's later than I thought.
We need to head toward the contest area." When they
arrived at the designated spot, Avery took the podium,
thanked everyone for attending and asked all contest
participants to head toward the open area near the base-
ball field.

At eleven o'clock, on the dot, she called forward the
first contestants in the best-dressed category, a girl
named Eva and her shih tzu, dressed in a pink tutu.
"Are you a dancer?"

"Tiffany and I both like to dance." Then she and
her pet demonstrated. The dog stood on her hind legs,

bounced a little and then twirled, while her owner pirouetted beside her.

The crowd clapped, and Avery asked the pair to parade before the judges' table.

When they reached Reed, he smiled, scribbled notes on the sheet in front of him, and said, "You two are great dancers."

Next, Avery called forward Mrs. Russell and Chandra. The toy poodle wore a white wedding dress complete with a veil and tiara. "Now, this is a dress any bride would envy," Avery said into the microphone.

"I had so much fun making this for Chandra. My neighbor Eleanor was going to bring her poodle, Max. I made him a tux and top hat, but she had another engagement."

The crowd laughed at Mrs. Russell's choice of words.

"That's too bad. I'm sure Chandra and Max make a beautiful couple. Now, if you'll walk over to the judges—"

"We know the routine, dear."

Avery smiled as the elderly woman sauntered to the judges' table, Chandra following, her silk train trailing behind her.

"Mrs. Russell, the dress is amazing. Chandra looks radiant," Reed said when the pair reached him.

As Avery called forward the last contestant, Jacob, a young boy dressed in a Broncos jersey, and his dog, Harry, a Lab mix wearing a similar shirt, she smiled at how Reed was throwing himself into the spirit of the contests. Who would've figured? After chatting with the boy, she sent him to parade in front of the judges.

"I'm a big Broncos fan, too. Who's your favorite player?" Reed asked.

"Von Miller," Jacob said. Then he frowned. "I don't stand a chance of winning against that wedding dress."

"Chandra's a tough act to beat for best-dressed." Reed tilted his head toward Harper and the other judge, a high-school cheerleader. "Especially with two female judges."

The boy nodded in male understanding.

Avery drifted closer to better hear the conversation.

"There's still the pet-lookalike contest. I think you'd stand a good chance in that one."

When the young boy beamed, Avery's heart swelled. She'd always known Reed had a soft heart. He didn't see it, but actions like this told Avery that he'd be a good father.

Minutes later, after she'd announced that Chandra was the winner of the best-dressed contest, she saw Jacob talking to Emma—she hoped about entering the lookalike contest. Mrs. Russell gushed over her prize, a gift certificate for a portrait of Chandra in her winning costume, provided by the airbrush artist at the event.

When Emma brought her the contestant list for the lookalike contest, Avery saw Jacob's name. Despite some tough competition from a bald man and his bulldog, Jacob and Harry ended up walking away with the win and a basket full of dog treats and toys donated by the Pet Palace.

When the contests were over, Avery reminded the crowd about the Frisbee-catching exhibition and K-9 police dog demonstrations. The day couldn't have been going any better.

"Baxter! Come back!" Carly shouted.

Avery closed her eyes. She'd jinxed it.

She glanced toward the vendor area. People scrambled on the pathway to catch Baxter or get out of his way, she didn't know which. The sound of raised voices and dogs barking, punctuated with periodic screams, grew deafening as she raced toward the bedlam.

"The escape artist is here?" Reed asked as he raced beside her.

"We've got to catch him before anyone gets hurt or we have a dog fight on our hands."

Visions of lawsuits danced in her head.

"We'll get him." Reed assured her.

"Look for his bright orange Adopt Me vest."

"I see him," Reed said. "Go right, toward the Pet Palace booth."

She ran, calling Baxter's name.

"Baxter, come!" Reed's booming voice, ringing with authority, cut through the turmoil.

Avery stared in disbelief as the blasted dog froze, turned their way and calmly trotted toward them. When Baxter reached them, he lunged for Reed.

"Sit," Reed commanded as he grabbed the dog's leash.

The dog plopped down beside Reed and shoved his black nose into Reed's hand, his tail creating a decent breeze as it wagged.

"Wow, how'd you do that?" a breathless Carly asked when she joined them. "He won't listen to anyone, especially when he's on the lam."

Reed shrugged. "Beats me. Dogs don't usually like me."

But Avery knew. There was something in Baxter that connected with Reed. They didn't know much about the dog's past. The police had brought him in as a stray. His shaggy coat had been so matted they'd had to completely shave him. He'd been a good ten pounds underweight and somewhat standoffish, but something about

Baxter had tugged at the staff's hearts. She thought about what her mother had said: *that boy's been running for years.* That was it. Both Reed and Baxter had survived tough pasts. Avery bit her lip as tears filled her eyes. What would it take for Reed to stop running?

"I'm sorry, Avery. You were right. I never should've brought Baxter." Carly reached for the leash.

Baxter whined and pressed himself against Reed's thigh.

"I'll take him back to the shelter." This time when Carly reached for the leash, Baxter barked.

"Stop it," Reed snapped, and the dog quieted. "I'll get him to the van."

"I don't know, Reed," Avery said.

"Trust me."

His low voice ricocheted through her. This was more about them than it was about Baxter. Reed's gaze, open and yet beseeching, tugged at her heart.

Trust him? If she loved him, how could she not trust him? She nodded. "I do."

As Reed walked beside Avery, Baxter trotting alongside them, he realized he'd seen a different side of her today. They actually had more in common workwise than he'd thought.

Through watching her, he remembered what life could be like as part of a close-knit community. He'd actually enjoyed talking with the townspeople there, and they'd seemed genuinely interested in his life since leaving Estes Park. The pity he'd seen in people's eyes growing up had been absent today. He'd felt almost as if he belonged.

Because of Avery.

"I don't know how we're ever going to get this guy

adopted now." She glared at the dog, who appeared oblivious to her irritation. "You'll be forever known as the holy terror who ran amok at the Pet Walk."

"You really think he won't find a home?"

"I've always said there's a person for every dog. It just takes a while sometimes, but he's been here so long already. He's been returned once and now this."

"How long do you give him before you—" He couldn't bring himself to say the words.

"We're a no-kill shelter, so he won't be euthanized, but staying so long isn't good for an animal. Volunteers interact with them, but after a while they can become depressed."

He stared at the mutt, who responded by wagging his tail. Jess had been right. There was something about this dog.

Don't look to me for help, buddy. Hit up some other guy. I've got enough problems.

"How about I take you out to dinner tonight?" Reed said, needing to change the subject.

Avery frowned. "I'd love to, but after we're done cleaning up here, we have to count the money, do some preliminary accounting and prepare the bank deposit."

He leaned down and kissed her lightly. "I'll be waiting when you're done."

LATER THAT AFTERNOON, Avery sat at her desk with the shelter's bookkeeper, Mary Beth, reconciling pledges and preparing the bank deposit. Piles of checks, cash and Pet Walk paperwork were spread out in front of them.

"Do you have the numbers yet? How did we do?" Emma poked her head inside the office door.

"Once Mary Beth gets the donation jar money tallied, we'll have the totals."

"Look who I found knocking at the back door." Emma stepped aside and Reed materialized in the doorway, a take-out food bag in his hands.

"I know Avery didn't eat much at the event, so I brought dinner for everyone." He walked across her office and placed the sack on her credenza. The spicy tang of barbecue filled the room. "I'll even play waiter. We've got barbecue-beef sandwiches, coleslaw, potato salad and baked beans."

He asked what each one of them wanted, dished up their orders and brought the food to their desks. Avery smiled as she thanked Reed. She could get used to this kind of pampering.

After they'd finished eating, Mary Beth reached down by her feet and picked up a plastic container that had once held dog treats but was now covered with paper emblazoned with the shelter logo and the word *Donations* in big letters. She unscrewed the lid and dumped the contents out in front of her. Coins plinked as they spilled out onto the wooden desktop. Bills rustled against checks. While the bookkeeper separated that money, Avery returned to tallying the pledge amounts and Emma went to call the raffle winners.

"What else can I do?" Reed asked after he'd cleared away the remnants of their meal.

"You don't have to stick around," Avery said.

"I want to see how you guys did today." Then he tossed her a steamy look that said, *And the more I help, the sooner I can get you alone.*

Avery felt the heat rise to her cheeks as she grabbed the stack of checks to her left. "You could photocopy these for us."

He nodded and took the checks from her. "If you give me your bank stamp, I'll take care of that while I'm at it."

She reached into her desk, found the deposit stamp and handed that to him, as well.

"How's the chair working out?" he asked.

"It's amazing. Not only is it comfortable, but I feel so important sitting in it."

"You *are* important."

Her heart caught at his words. But how important was she? Important enough for him to stick around once his brother returned? Important enough to give her a child?

"Hey, you two. I'm still here, you know," Mary Beth teased.

Avery felt herself blush more. How could she have forgotten that she and Reed weren't alone? The man sure messed with her focus.

Reed mumbled a quick apology and shot out of the office, his cheeks a little red as well, while Avery returned to reconciling pledges. A few minutes later, Mary Beth said, "I've got the donation-jar total for you, Avery—$832.75."

Avery added the amount to her spreadsheet, clicked, and the total amount popped onto the screen. She patted her hands on her desk. "Drum roll—$60,213.45! We did it! We raised enough for the down payment."

Emma ran into the office shouting and hugged Mary Beth. Reed rushed in, too, and swept Avery up in his arms. "I knew you'd do it. I'm so proud of you."

They'd saved the shelter. She was in love with a wonderful man. Life couldn't get much better.

Chapter Twelve

Reed and Jess settled into a pattern. A couple of nights a week they ate dinner with Avery and Nannette at the McAlister ranch. He'd started volunteering at the shelter again with Jess, but this time he did so unquestioningly, with a smile.

Since today hadn't been their day to volunteer, after he picked up Jess from school they'd come straight home. Now she was holed up in her room working on homework, while he got a little more work done before starting dinner.

Even work was leveling out. Customers had grown accustomed to working with him via Skype, and Ethan had settled in to his new duties. A week had gone by since Reed had received a panicked, the-sky's-falling phone call from him.

Then it hit him. He'd been happier the past few weeks than he'd ever been. Not just content, but downright silly and filled-with-hope happy. And he was in love.

But what about the future? Could he give Avery what she needed in life, what she deserved? His cell phone rang, interrupting his thoughts. Vowing he wouldn't worry about that now when he had months to figure things out, he answered the call.

"Ethan approached me about a job," Blake Dunston, Reed's key software engineer on the SiEtch project, said. "He insists you're on the wrong track with this product, and you've misjudged the market. He's starting a new company to make a cheaper version of SiEtch. He claims he's got copies of the software and the hardware specs on his home computer. He plans on starting there and modifying what we've done to create his product."

Reed's breathing accelerated. His hands started sweating as he tried to process what had happened. His best friend, the man he'd built his business with, had betrayed him.

As if that wasn't bad enough, if word about his actions got out, and Reed had indeed been wrong about the market, this could ruin his business. And here he was in Colorado, thousands of miles away from it all. Rage boiled inside him. If he ever got his hands on Ethan...

He'd what? Beat the hell out of him like he had his dad?

A headache bloomed between Reed's eyes. He and Ethan had gone around the issue like dogs chasing their tails. Unfortunately, nothing he said changed Ethan's shortsighted opinion that product cost was the key factor, while Reed emphasized the need for 3-D transistor capacity. That's what would set their product apart from others in the market. The discussion had ended when he said RJ Instruments was his company, as was the decision on how to proceed.

He realized their relationship had changed once he became Ethan's boss. The more his company grew, the more distant they became. But to betray him like this? After all the years they'd worked together?

"Has he approached anyone else?"

"Word is he offered Tom Merrick a job, too," Blake replied.

It figured Ethan would want the project's key hardware developer on board.

"What did you tell him when he offered you the job?"

"I said I needed to talk to my wife tonight before I gave him an answer. Then I called you."

Good. That gave him a day before Ethan got wind something was up. "I won't forget this, Blake, and I'll make my thanks more tangible after I've dealt with it."

Reed's hands shook as he speed-dialed his lawyer's number. He quickly detailed his conversation with Blake. "What can I do to stop him?"

"I'll file for a temporary injunction in civil court. You need to contact the San Francisco district attorney and file a criminal complaint because he's stealing company assets."

Reed grabbed a pen and paper from the desk and started taking notes. "Do you think we can get the injunction?"

"We'll need affidavits from Blake and Tom for the civil hearing. Those, plus the fact that we've got a patent pending on the product and Ethan signed a no-competition clause, all strengthen our case."

Immediately after ending his call with his lawyer, Reed contacted the district attorney, who told him they'd be happy to file charges. The catch? He had to appear in person and the appointment was tomorrow morning.

What was he going to do about Jess? Today was Tuesday. He hated to pull her out of school, especially since she had a math test tomorrow. But what other option did he have? Avery.

He punched in her cell number, but had to leave a

message. "A major problem's come up at work. I've
got to fly to California. I should only be gone a day or
two. Can Jess stay with you until I get back? Call me
when you get this."

AVERY HEARD HER PHONE RING, but as she was in the barn
examining Twin Creeks' new foal under the watchful,
nervous eye of his mother, she let the call go to voice
mail. After she finished the animal's exam and cleaned
up, she settled onto the couch with a glass of iced tea
to check her messages, but before she could, the door-
bell sounded.

When she answered the front door, Jess, her eyes red
and swollen, burst into tears.

"What's wrong?" Avery rushed forward and enveloped the girl in a hug. For a minute Jess clung to Avery
and sobbed. Her wrenching cries tore at Avery's heart
as she rubbed the girl's back. "Is it your dad? Did you
get bad news?"

*Please, don't let it be that. This dear child won't sur-
vive losing him, too.*

"Dad's fine. It's Uncle Reed," Jess croaked out.

Avery's heart rocked. Had something happened to
him? She forced the words out. "Is he okay?"

A new wave of sobs gushed forth. Avery held Jess
tighter. "You've got to calm down enough to tell me
what's wrong. I can't help unless I know what happened."

"Can I stay here?"

"Of course."

All teenage bravado stripped from her gaze, Jess's
eyes screamed of her anguish. Whatever had happened
was bad. Very bad.

Avery forced herself to remain calm as she ushered

Jess into the living room. Despite her urge to bombard
the teenager with questions, she patted the couch beside her and grabbed a calming breath before saying,
"Tell me what happened."

Jess melted onto the couch, dropping her backpack
at her feet. "I just talked to my grandparents. They got
approval for me to live with them in Florida until Dad
gets back."

Reed was okay. The fist squeezing Avery's heart
loosened. This she could deal with. "I know they love
you very much, but just because they have the okay and
want you to live with them doesn't mean you have to."

Tears welled up in Jess's soft brown eyes. "They said
to thank Uncle Reed. He contacted a reporter. He said if
they didn't let me stay with my grandparents while Dad
was gone, the whole world would find out they weren't
supporting a serviceman fighting for his country."

Avery's heart rebelled against the thought. Reed
wouldn't do that. He'd promised Colt he'd take care of
Jess. He knew she'd threatened to run away if she was
forced to move in with her grandparents.

*Taking care of her and running my business long-
distance is tougher than I expected.*

No. He'd changed since he made that comment at
Halligan's weeks ago. Jess mattered to him. They both
mattered to him.

"He doesn't want me." Jess's pain emanated from
her in waves, mirroring Avery's.

Avery's mind spun as she processed everything.
Nothing made sense. She'd seen the difference between
Reed and Jess. Genuine love existed between them. He
couldn't fake a relationship that well.

But how well do you really know him? He was gone

for years, and hasn't been back that long. Don't go there now. What's important is helping Jess.

Avery shut off her own emotions. "I know he loves you very much."

"Then why would he want to get rid of me?"

"Have you talked to him about this?"

Jess shook her head. "I left and came here."

Hope, tiny and fragile, sprouted inside her. Avery wouldn't assume the worst. She'd give Reed the benefit of the doubt until she spoke with him.

"Things aren't always what they seem. Talk to him. Maybe there's been a misunderstanding. Reporters often have an agenda. Maybe your grandparents heard what they wanted to hear. Give your uncle a chance to explain."

Please let it be that he contacted the reporter weeks ago and forgot to stop what he'd put in motion once his circumstances and feelings changed.

"What's the point?" Jess scooped up a decorative pillow off the couch, hugging it close to her chest. "He'll either tell me he doesn't want me or he'll lie about it. No matter what he has to say, I don't want to hear it." Her lip quivered. "What's wrong with me? First my mom ran off. She never even told me she was leaving."

"Don't *ever* think your mother leaving was your fault. I didn't know her well, but my guess is she had—" Avery paused. *Your mother had severe problems and was a selfish, unfeeling bitch.* She swallowed her anger. "Your mom and dad had problems. Plus she was dealing with other issues that had nothing to do with you. That's why she left."

And if she'd given a rat's ass about anyone but herself she'd have told you it wasn't your fault before she skipped town with her lover.

"Then Dad left for Afghanistan, and now Uncle Reed wants to get rid of me."

"Your dad didn't have a choice. That's his job."

"If he really loved me, he'd get a different one so he could stick around."

Jess had a valid point, but admitting the fact wouldn't help the teenager now.

"When your dad gets home you need to tell him how you feel. I bet once he knows how much you need him around, he'll resign from the National Guard."

"That's months away. What can I do now? I can't live with my grandparents. I love them, but I'll die if I have to live with all those old people. I won't know anyone at school. I won't have any friends. They don't even have internet access, so I can't Skype or talk to anyone on Facebook." The longer Jess talked, the more frantic her speech became. "I'll run away. That's what I'll do."

"Whoa. Slow down." Avery placed her hand over Jess's and squeezed. "Breathe. I want you to—"

"I won't live with my grandparents in an old folks' neighborhood."

"The first step is to talk to your uncle."

"Can't I live here with you and your mom? I won't be any trouble, I promise. I can do all the cooking and cleaning. I'll earn my keep."

Avery bit her lip. She wouldn't cry. Jess needed a calm and in-control adult. "You know we'd love for you to stay with us, but it's not that simple. Your uncle Reed is your legal guardian. We'd need his approval and your dad's, but I think we're getting ahead of ourselves. The first thing you need to do is talk to your uncle. Be honest with him. Tell him what your grandparents said and that you don't want to live with them. See what he says."

"What if he doesn't care what I want?"

Then I'll pound some sense into him.

"I care, and so does my mom. We'll do whatever we can." Her cell phone rang, and she glanced at the screen. "It's the shelter. I need to make sure it's nothing important."

When she answered the call, Emma said animal control had picked up a stray that had been hit by a car. She was fairly certain its leg was broken, but added it might need to be amputated. Though Emma wasn't a vet, she'd seen enough similar cases to offer a reliable assessment. "Have Carly take X-rays. I'm on my way." She ended the call and explained the situation to Jess. "I need to go into the shelter. Why don't you come with me?"

"Can I stay here instead? I don't want to see anyone now."

"You shouldn't be alone."

"Isn't your mom around?"

Avery glanced at her watch. "She's at book club. She'll be home in an hour or so."

"I'll be fine. Go."

Avery sat there, torn. "I could call Doc Brown to see if he could fill in for me."

"I don't need a babysitter."

Now she'd insulted Jess. It was only for an hour. She could text her mom, explain things and ask her to come home sooner. "When I'm done at the shelter, we'll talk to your uncle together. Everything will be all right. I promise you won't have to live with your grandparents if you don't want to."

She'd make sure. No matter what she had to do.

An hour later, Avery returned to the ranch. While the dog's leg was broken, it wasn't a bad enough break to require amputation. She'd splinted the leg, left Carly with instructions to watch the animal and call if anything changed, and made a quick exit before anyone else sidetracked her.

As she climbed out of her truck, her mom pulled up beside her. She was just getting home now? "You didn't get my text about what happened with Reed?"

"I shut my phone off at book club. I guess I forgot to turn it back on."

Avery explained about the call Jess had received from her grandparents and how she'd left her at the ranch alone. Then she raced up the walkway, unlocked the front door and burst inside, yelling Jess's name.

Silence. What had she done? Panic jolted through Avery, making her heart slam against her ribs. "She's not answering me, Mom. What if she did something silly? I never should've left her alone."

Worry lined her mother's face. "I'll check in the barn. You search the house."

Five minutes later, they met in the kitchen, neither one having found any trace of Jess. "I've got a bad feeling about this. She took her backpack."

"That doesn't mean anything. She takes that thing everywhere, even to the shelter," Nannette said. "She's probably at a friend's house, or maybe she went home to talk to Reed."

"You didn't see the hurt in her eyes. What if she ran away like she threatened to do when her dad talked to her about living with her grandparents? I should've made her come to the shelter with me."

Nannette gave Avery a quick hug. "You can't undo the past, so quit stewing over it. You go to the Rocking M. See if she's there with Reed. Since she's mentioned her friends a few times, I'll start making calls."

As Avery drove through Estes Park, she alternated between saying prayers that they'd find Jess and re-

minding herself that she couldn't deck Reed the minute he opened the door for setting this mess in motion.

"Did you get my message?" he asked when he opened
the door. Dressed in black slacks, a white button-down
shirt and his expensive loafers, he looked the way he
had when he'd first returned to Estes Park.

"What message?"

"I found out that my vice president of engineering,
the guy I left in charge, stole my company's latest product and is planning to start his own company. I need
to fly to California to file charges with the San Francisco district attorney. Then I've got to obtain affidavits
from the employees he offered jobs to for the temporary injunction hearing. Can Jess stay with you for a
few days?"

"Then she's here?"

He nodded. "She's in her room. I was about to tell
her dinner's ready."

"Thank God. I was so worried when I came home
and she wasn't there. Have you two talked? She was so
upset when I saw her."

"What? Why's Jess upset? She was fine when I
picked her up from school." Worry and confusion filled
Reed's gaze.

Jess was here, but they hadn't talked? The hairs on
the back of Avery's neck stood up. Something wasn't
right. She tore through the hallway shouting Jess's
name. "Which room is hers?"

"First door on the left," Reed said from behind her.
"What's wrong?"

Not bothering to knock, she burst into the room,
finding it empty. She faced Reed. "You didn't even
know she was gone? When was the last time you saw
her?"

"After we got home I went into the office to work, and she went to her room."

"School ended at three-twenty. She showed up at my house at four in tears." Avery glanced at her watch. "That was almost two hours ago. How could you do this to Jess? How could you hurt her like this when she loves you so much?"

"What do you think I did?"

"Her grandparents called. They said to thank you for getting the homeowners' association to make an exception for Jess to live with them. Tell me it's not true. Tell me you didn't want to dump her on her grandparents."

Tell me you weren't leaving me, too.

"Wait a minute. I put that in motion weeks ago. I'd forgotten about it."

"How could you even think about doing that when you knew how she felt about living in a retirement community?" Avery's voice rose with her anger. "You knew she'd threatened to run away, and you didn't care. How could you be so callous?"

"I'm not. Colt and I talked about this. He knew how nervous I was about making mistakes with Jess. He said if Jess agreed, he was okay with her staying with her grandparents. I didn't even know the approval came through, and if I had, I'd have talked to her. I never would've made her go to Florida if she didn't want to."

What he said sounded so reasonable, so logical, but could she believe him? Would Jess? "We've got to find her. I really think she's run away."

REED MASSAGED THE KNOT that had formed in his neck. Damn. How could everything hit the fan at once? He needed to leave for Denver soon or he wouldn't make his flight. The longer it took him to reach California, the more time elapsed before legal measures went into place. His business, his livelihood, all he had was on the line right now. His employees' livelihoods hung in the balance, as well.

"Slow down. You could be jumping to conclusions." His heart raced as he worked to logically assess the situation. He scanned Jess's room searching for any noticeable changes. Clothes lay scattered across the floor and on various pieces of furniture. The place looked like the same disaster zone. "Jess can't have run away. Look. All of her stuff's still here."

The rattle of dog tags sounded behind them in the hallway, and his heart rate slowed. He turned and, for the first time since he'd arrived, was genuinely glad to see Thor. Thank God the mutt was still here. "Jess wouldn't leave Thor if she ran away. She's probably at a friend's house."

"We've got to call the police," Avery insisted.

"They'll ask if we've contacted all her friends and where we've searched." He pulled out his cell phone and called his niece. After four rings, her voice mail kicked in. "Jess, I heard your grandparents called. Let me explain what happened. Call me as soon as you get this message. It's not what you think."

He turned to Avery. "Colt has a couple of PTA directories in his desk. We can use those to call people to find out if anyone's seen her."

Once back in the office, he dug around in the top drawer and pulled out two small purple booklets. "I'll take last year's. She's talked to you more about her friends than she has me." He handed the other booklet to Avery. "It'll take me an hour and a half to get to the airport. When I get there I'll call to see what you've discovered, and I'll make more calls. That is, if we haven't heard from Jess by then."

"You're still going?" Avery shook her head as disappointment hardened her gaze.

"I have to. The D.A. said I have to file charges in person. I've got an appointment first thing in the morning. Having criminal charges in the works will strengthen my case for the injunction. My company's invested a lot of money and time in the SiEtch project. Losing it could bankrupt me, and put all my employees out of work. I've got some money saved, so I'd be fine, but not everyone does."

"I'll find Jess. I've come to love that girl, you know. I defended you to her. I told her that she was wrong, that you loved her—"

"I do."

"If you did, you'd have been out the door to search before I finished telling you what had happened. I thought you'd changed. I was a fool to fall in love with you again."

"You love me?" Joy burst through him, white-hot and blinding.

"The man I love would never do this to Jess. She feels you abandoned her just like her mother did. You're not the man I thought you were." Avery stormed to the front door.

"Avery, that's not fair." He reached out to her, but she stepped away.

"Go to California. I hope everything works out with your business. I hope it fills the hole deep inside you."

"I don't have a choice. If I don't go, I could lose everything."

"You don't get it, do you? You've already lost everything that matters."

Chapter Thirteen

Thirty minutes outside town, the words Avery had hurled at him pounded in his head, leaving Reed with a massive headache. He kept telling himself that Jess hadn't run away. She couldn't have gone far without her clothes and Thor. He had time to make things right with her once he ensured his business wouldn't go belly-up. Then he could fix things with Avery.

He had to save his business. People counted on him to protect their jobs. It was all he had.

It was all he had?

If he died tomorrow, who'd show up at his funeral? Colt and Jess, if her father tied her up and hauled her to the service. Some of his employees would come, but how well did he know any of them? What a damned sorry commentary on his life.

Was that what he wanted at the end of his life? To look back and have nothing to show for himself but a company?

He thought about his mom, how much he'd loved her and how she'd always encouraged him. When she'd died, he'd been angry at her for leaving him and Colt alone to cope with their father. He'd raged against her, wondering if she'd left his father things would've been different. She'd been the only one who had thought he could take on the world. The only one other than Colt who believed in him.

Until Avery.

What the hell had he done? He'd been running for years. He realized now, trying to prove something to a man who, even when he'd been alive, hadn't possessed the ability to love or approve of anyone.

His father was long cold in the grave, but he still controlled Reed's life and his choices.

How could he throw away what he had with Avery and Jess?

If his business failed, he could start over. He could get a job. Hell, he could move in with Colt and put his energy into making the Rocking M the best damned horse ranch in the country. He had options, and he'd pull any and every string he could to see that his employees found jobs, too. His business wasn't everything.

Avery and Jess were his life. Family. That's what mattered. What lasted. Avery had helped him, even when he'd been a complete ass. She'd been there for him...smoothing things over with Jess.

All those years ago when he'd desperately wanted and needed a family, he'd never seen that he had one. With Avery. Her family took him in. Her parents treated him the way they did their own children. They'd encouraged him, supported him and helped him through the worst time in his life. He'd had everything he'd ever wanted with Avery, and he'd thrown it all away because he'd been afraid he'd turn into his father.

His mother had let fear rule her life. Fear of his father. Fear of living on her own and having to provide for her sons had kept her with an abusive man. Reed refused to live that way any longer.

He turned into a gas-station parking lot. He had to get back home. The word rattled around in his head. Estes Park, home? The thought ricocheted through him. It *was* home, and he was in love with Avery. Hell, he'd probably never stopped loving her.

He knew that he wanted her in his life—forever.

As he pulled back onto the highway to head home, he prayed it wasn't too late to undo the damage he'd done with both her and Jess.

AVERY AND HER MOTHER CALLED everyone they could think of, and no one had seen Jess since school ended. They'd enlisted the rest of the McAlisters to search. Even Maggie with little Michaela in her stroller went around town asking businesses if they'd seen Jess. The longer they went without finding a trace of the teenager, the more certain Avery became that she'd run away.

Her panic and her anger multiplied. How could Reed have left for California? Couldn't he see that the trouble with his company was nothing compared to the situation with Jess?

He insisted they weren't sure Jess had run away. They might not have been then, but Avery was positive now. When she talked with him later, if he wouldn't call the police, then she would, and she'd contact Colt. She'd do whatever she had to in order to find Jess before something happened to her.

Oh, Lord. A devastated fourteen-year-old girl on the run. A predator or pimp's prime dream.

Her cell phone rang.

"Any news?" Reed asked.

"Nothing. My family's been searching since you left. No one's seen Jess since school got out."

"What about Lindsey?" Reed's voice broke. "Have you talked to her?"

Tears pooled in her eyes and she bit her lip to keep from crying. "They haven't spoken much since Jess started volunteering at the shelter, but I tried her, too."

"I'm on my way back. I'll be there in half an hour, tops. It's going to be tough reaching Colt. Contact the National Guard for help with that. After I talk to my brother, I'll call the police and ask them to issue an Amber Alert."

Reed was coming back. Maybe he wasn't a lost cause.

When she met him at the door twenty minutes later, she found his face drawn, features tight.

"You came back for Jess."

"Not just for her. I couldn't leave things like they were between us, either. Nothing matters if I don't have you in my life." He stepped inside and wrapped his arms around her, and her anger disappeared as the need to comfort him washed over her. Whatever was or wasn't between them, they'd deal with it later when Jess was safe.

"Reed, I'm so worried."

He stepped away. "Me, too. She's such a wonderful kid, and I hurt her so badly."

She recognized the pain in his eyes. He *had* changed. Looking into his anguish-filled eyes, she knew he finally saw things from Jess's viewpoint.

"A chaplain's waiting for your call. He'll put you in touch with Colt via Skype."

Reed nodded as she led him into the ranch office. Looking at him seated behind the massive oak desk that had once belonged to her father, she remembered what he'd said about the last time he'd been in this room.

Now here he was, his life in turmoil again. She scooted an armchair closer to the desk as he waited to connect with his brother.

"Colt, I've screwed things up with Jess." Reed told his brother about his conversation with the reporter. "I don't know what happened, but the association changed their minds, and I never got word. Your in-laws called Jess before I had a chance to explain things to her. It looks like she ran away."

Weariness and guilt lined Reed's face. His shoulders hunched. Avery placed her hand over his and squeezed, wishing she could do more.

"Don't beat yourself up," Colt said. "It's as much my fault as yours. I told you I was okay with what you were doing. Just find her."

"Do you know anywhere she might have gone?"

"You've checked with all her friends?" Colt asked, fear similar to his brother's evident on his face.

"Avery's called everyone she can think of, and her family's searched the town. No one's seen Jess since school. Is there anyone she'd confide in?"

Avery leaned closer to the screen. "Colt, there has to be something we're missing. Something we haven't thought of. Does Jess have any friends we might not know about? A friend she met at camp or somewhere like that?"

"That's it." Reed beamed at her. His hand covered hers, and squeezed. "Colt, when we talked on the phone that first time, you said Jess's best friend moved soon after Lynn died. Where does she live?"

"Hannah's in Chicago."

Adrenaline coursed through Reed, shoving aside his panic. He knew where Jess was. Knew it in his gut.

"And Jess has the credit card you gave her in case of emergency."

While he asked his brother where he kept the account information, Avery opened the drawer in front of her and retrieved paper and pen. Then she jotted down the information Colt gave them.

"I'm at Avery's right now. When I get the company's phone number, I'll call to see if Jess booked a flight. That'll be quicker than trying to find her computer and tracing it that way."

"And the airport wouldn't think twice about a teenager flying alone, especially because only ticketed passengers can go to the gate," Avery added.

"I pray you're right," Colt said, his voice shaking with emotion.

"I'll let you know what we find out."

Five minutes later, they were in Colt's office and Reed was on the phone with the credit-card company. He learned Jess had purchased a one-way ticket to Chicago.

"Jess booked a nine-forty flight to Chicago." Reed called information and asked for the Denver police department's number. His heart drummed painfully in his chest as he prayed Jess had arrived at the airport in one piece. A lot of things could happen to a young girl alone between Estes Park and Denver. While she acted all tough and self-sufficient, working with Jess at the shelter and watching her with Avery had shown him her kind heart. She could be so trusting. What if someone preyed on that?

His hand shook as he laced his fingers with Avery's. She peered up at him, when she asked, "What if something's happened to her? What if some nutcase found her?"

"Jess is a smart girl. The situation with her friends and the court taught her a lot about blindly trusting people. She'd be cautious."

He prayed he was right. When the police answered, he explained the situation and gave the officer Jess's flight information. He turned to Avery. "I'm on hold. They're calling airport security to see if she's there."

He squeezed Avery's hand as elevator music filled his ears. What if they didn't find her? He placed his phone on the smooth mahogany desk and put it on Speaker. Whatever they learned, he wanted Avery to hear it firsthand.

"The airline shows she boarded the plane," said the voice over the phone. "Security is on the way to remove her from the flight. They'll hold her until you get there. We're sending an officer, as well."

Reed started shaking and tears filled his eyes as the stranglehold on his heart loosened. After he ended the call, he grabbed Avery. He held her for a minute as relief flowed through his veins. Jess hadn't paid the price for his stupidity. "Right after I hug the daylights out of her, I'm going to blister her ears. How could she put herself in such danger by going to Denver alone?"

Avery's tears soaked his shirt. He kissed her temple and released her. "Call your family and the chaplain so he can contact Colt. Tell them we've found Jess. I'm heading to the Denver airport to get her."

"I'm coming, too."

He swiped a hand across his eyes. Things could have turned out so differently. Apparently God did, indeed, as his mother used to say, protect fools and children. At least, He had this time.

ONCE ON THE ROAD TO DENVER, Avery called her mother and the chaplain with the news that they'd located Jess. When she finished those tasks, Reed said, "I meant what I said. Nothing matters—success, money, my company, none of it—if I don't have you in my life. I love you. I want to spend the rest of my life with you, marry you, but—"

"Yes." Joy burst within her as tears spilled down her cheeks. She thought she'd gotten over him, that she'd stopped loving him, but she hadn't. She'd merely buried her emotions and quit feeling much of anything. She'd given up on men and on love.

"Are you sure? I'm a mirror image of my father. What if we're alike in more ways than just our looks?" His hands tightened on the steering wheel and a vein throbbed wildly in his neck. "I nearly beat him to death. What if I lose control like that again? You're so wonderful. Your family's great. The kind that accepts everyone who walks in the door. I don't deserve you."

"That's what this is all about? You're worried you're not good enough for me?"

Reed nodded.

"May I get down from the pedestal please?" Avery asked.

"What are you talking about?"

"You've put me on a pedestal, and that's not where I want to be. I'd rather walk along beside you."

"I spent so much of my life being angry. At my mother for not leaving my father, for dying. At my father for being such a bastard. Since being back here, what I've been feeling scares me."

"Have I ever made you angry?"

He smiled for the first time since Jess had gone missing. "Is that a rhetorical question?"

She chucked. "Exactly. In all those times, I never once worried you'd hurt me. Then there was the night at the police station. You were so mad at Jess, but you never lifted a hand toward her."

"I thought about it."

"The important thing is you *didn't*. Why can't you see that? Why can't you see what I do? A good, caring man desperate to do right by his niece and everyone else around him."

"Because I don't know what I would've done if you hadn't been there."

"You wouldn't have hurt Jess." Her voice rang with her certainty. She longed to hold him, to reassure him, but all she could do was rub his arm. The man wasn't capable of violence. "If you think about it, deep down you know that. Your father attacked you. Did you fear for your life?"

"I don't know. Maybe. All I remember is that I couldn't take the beatings anymore."

"You were defending yourself. If my father did to me what your dad did to you, I'd react the same way. I might not have the physical strength to beat him, but I'd hit him with whatever I could get my hands on, and I wouldn't stop until he didn't get up. Does that make you scared that I'll hurt you?"

"It's not the same."

"Your father isn't the only one who makes up who you are. Did you get your business sense from him? Is that where you got your negotiating skills?"

He paused. His gaze focused on the road stretched out in front of them. "I remember one day before Mom died. While she was cooking dinner, Colt and I were sitting at the kitchen table working on homework. When Colt had trouble with his math, she came over to help him. She said he had to keep trying because getting a good education was important. She told us she wished she'd finished college, and that she'd dreamed of owning a clothing boutique, but she quit school to support her parents when her father became sick and lost his job."

He'd lost his mother so long ago. He carried childhood memories that probably had been overwhelmed by his dominant, unyielding father. Avery remembered his mother. Always smiling, she'd been genuine, affectionate and giving. All things Reed had to shut off to survive once she died.

"Your business skills came from your mother. She's in you, too, though you don't realize it. You have her kind heart. You've done so much for me and for the shelter. You've worked hard to get to know Jess. You've learned from your mistakes."

"How can you say that after today?"

"You screwed up. We all do."

"I still don't know about children. The chances of me continuing the cycle of violence—"

"Did Colt beat his wife or Jess?"

"I'm not my brother."

"And you're not your father. I can't believe you're afraid of a baby. You've been thrown into the deep end of the pool parenting-wise with a teenager, and you're scared of a baby? Plus, you'll have Griffin to turn to for advice. We can babysit Michaela to practice. By the time we have children you'll be a pro."

He could either live his life in fear or he could take a risk, and end up having it all. "If you're willing to take a risk on me—"

"Isn't that what I've been saying?" Avery rolled her eyes. "Now, is your proposal still on the table?"

"If you'll have me, yes."

TWO HOURS LATER, when the police ushered Reed and Avery into a small security office in the airport, he still had no idea what he'd say to Jess.

For a minute, he stood in the doorway staring at her, looking tiny sitting in the industrial metal chair.

She refused to look at him. He deserved that.

He walked forward, settled in the chair beside her and glanced at Avery for a shot of courage. He took a deep breath and faced his niece. "Jess, I don't know what to say except I screwed up."

"You wanted to get rid of me."

"When your dad asked me to stay with you, I was so scared I'd mess up, or worse." He clutched his knees to keep his hands from shaking. "My father used to beat the hell out of me."

"And Dad?"

Reed nodded. "Your father was the best big brother. He protected me when he could, and I can't tell you how many times he pulled me away before my dad and I could really go at it. One night after your dad moved away, my dad hit me. I nearly beat him to death. I was scared I might flip out one day and hurt you, too."

The ache in his chest eased. Letting go of the secrets he'd carried for so long felt freeing. "I had my lawyer working on getting your grandparents' Association of Homeowners to make an exception for you to live there before I left California. I really believed that was best for you, but I never would've forced you to go live with them if you didn't want to."

He wouldn't mention that Colt knew what he'd been doing. Jess didn't need to feel as if her father had been conspiring against her, too.

She still hadn't looked at him.

"I've made more mistakes dealing with you than I

have in my entire life. Talking to the reporter before I'd spoken with you was the biggest, but I'm willing to learn." He placed his hands over Jess's, and she finally glanced up at him.

Her soft brown eyes glistened with tears. *She's so young, and I hurt her so much.* "I love you, Jess. I always have. It took me a while to adjust to this stand-in-dad stuff, but now that I'm getting the hang of it, I like it."

She pulled her hands away from him and folded them in her lap. "Remember that day at the shelter when we were bathing Baxter?"

He nodded.

"I said if Dad died, I wouldn't have anyone. You told me I'd have you. You lied to me."

Her justifiable pain cut through him. "I said that after I talked with the reporter, and I meant it. I was so happy with you and Avery that I forgot I'd even spoken to her. I should've called her back and told her to forget about doing the story, but I didn't."

"What if you change your mind again?" Jess asked.

"You have no reason to trust me, but I won't change my mind. While I don't deserve a second chance, if you give me one, I'll do right by you. I'm willing to grovel if that'll help."

Jess smiled ever so slightly and then bit her lip. "It might."

"I was an ass."

"And I'll be happy to remind him of this if he ever starts acting like one again," Avery added from the other side of the room.

"What about my grandparents?"

"Now, listen up. I'm not going anywhere," Reed announced. "I'll explain things to them. Even if they eventually come to stay with you here, I'm not leaving. And if you want to keep living with me when that happens, I'll tell them that. You're stuck with me. Got it?"

Jess turned to Avery. "You're my witness."

"Count on it."

He knew he had a long way to go to regain Jess's trust, but at least she was giving him the opportunity. That was more than he deserved. "Now let's get out of here." Jess stood and he put one arm around her. Together they walked toward Avery. "Let's go home."

Avery clasped his hand. "Since we're at the airport, you should take the next flight to California. Save your business."

He shook his head. He had work to do at home with his family. "I'll contact the district attorney in the morning to see if he'll make an exception and start the paperwork without me being there."

"What have I missed?" Jess asked.

After he gave her a brief explanation of his business situation, she said, "Could we go with you? I've always wanted to see San Francisco."

"Don't you have a math test tomorrow?"

She nodded, disappointment filling her gaze. Then she pouted. "Maybe we can go some other time. I just wanted to spend some time with you."

He laughed, seeing through her ploy, but thrilled by her actions. "Just because I was a jerk before and have a lot to make up for doesn't mean you can pout and I'll be a pushover."

"You can't blame a girl for trying."

He glanced at the two females who filled his life with love. So what if she had a test? "I'll write school a note saying you were sick. After what's happened today, I'm not sure I want to let either one of you out of my sight."

LATER THAT WEEK when they returned from San Francisco, Avery couldn't help but smile as Jess regaled Nannette with the details of their trip. Reed stood on the patio grilling more burgers for the rest of her family, who were due to arrive any minute.

Her family.

She, Jess and Reed were just that. While he'd met with the district attorney to file charges, obtained the necessary affidavits and worked with his lawyer on a temporary injunction against Ethan, she and Jess had played tourists. They'd driven down Lombard Street, famous for its eight hairpin turns in one block. They'd visited Alcatraz, ridden the cable cars and seen the Golden Gate Bridge.

"Reed says we'll go back to San Francisco when we can stay longer, because he wants to show us all the stuff we didn't have time to see." Jess's face glowed with enthusiasm as she explained how she and Reed had picked out Avery's engagement ring.

Staring at the simple, but way too large, emerald-cut ring, Avery realized that the fact that selecting it had been a family affair made the ring even more special. She and Reed hadn't set a date yet. They both wanted Colt at their wedding. He'd be the best man, and she'd asked Jess to be her maid of honor.

Plus, Avery wanted Reed to take time to settle things with his business before they dived into wedding plans. His lawyer indicated that, with the testimony from his employees and the no-competition clause Ethan had signed, Reed wouldn't have any problem preventing his former friend from releasing a similar product. While in San Francisco he'd assembled his employees to discuss relocating to Estes Park. He said the company would pay relocation costs and give raises to those who wanted to move. For those who chose not to, he'd pay a year's severance and offer assistance in finding other work.

Reed materialized beside her and kissed Avery lightly on the lips. "A penny for your thoughts."

"That's all they're worth?"

"I gave you a ring, but you want me to ante up for your thoughts?"

She laughed.

"Baxter, no!" Jess yelled. "Uncle Reed, your dog ate my hamburger and now he's chasing Thor."

Reed shook his head and turned to Avery. "Those obedience classes can't start soon enough."

"The good news is he hasn't run away once since we brought him home from the shelter."

"The mutt knows a good thing when he's got one."

He bent and kissed her long and deeply. Her heart overflowed with love. Life couldn't be any better.

His hands framing her face, his gaze open and loving, he said, "Looks like Baxter and I are both done running."

* * * * *

REQUEST YOUR FREE BOOKS!
2 FREE NOVELS PLUS 2 FREE GIFTS!

 HARLEQUIN®

 American ★ Romance®

LOVE, HOME & HAPPINESS

YES! Please send me 2 FREE Harlequin® American Romance® novels and my 2 FREE gifts (gifts are worth about $10). After receiving them, if I don't wish to receive any more books, I can return the shipping statement marked "cancel." If I don't cancel, I will receive 4 brand-new novels every month and be billed just $4.49 per book in the U.S. or $5.24 per book in Canada. That's a savings of at least 14% off the cover price! It's quite a bargain! Shipping and handling is just 50¢ per book in the U.S. and 75¢ per book in Canada.* I understand that accepting the 2 free books and gifts places me under no obligation to buy anything. I can always return a shipment and cancel at any time. Even if I never buy another book, the two free books and gifts are mine to keep forever.

154/354 HDN FVPK

Name _____ (PLEASE PRINT) _____

Address _____ Apt. # _____

City _____ State/Prov. _____ Zip/Postal Code _____

Signature (if under 18, a parent or guardian must sign)

Mail to the **Harlequin® Reader Service:**
IN U.S.A.: P.O. Box 1867, Buffalo, NY 14240-1867
IN CANADA: P.O. Box 609, Fort Erie, Ontario L2A 5X3

Want to try two free books from another line?
Call 1-800-873-8635 or visit www.ReaderService.com.

* Terms and prices subject to change without notice. Prices do not include applicable taxes. Sales tax applicable in N.Y. Canadian residents will be charged applicable taxes. Offer not valid in Quebec. This offer is limited to one order per household. Not valid for current subscribers to Harlequin American Romance books. All orders subject to credit approval. Credit or debit balances in a customer's account(s) may be offset by any other outstanding balance owed by or to the customer. Please allow 4 to 6 weeks for delivery. Offer available while quantities last.

Your Privacy—The Harlequin® Reader Service is committed to protecting your privacy. Our Privacy Policy is available online at www.ReaderService.com or upon request from the Harlequin Reader Service.

We make a portion of our mailing list available to reputable third parties that offer products we believe may interest you. If you prefer that we not exchange your name with third parties, or if you wish to clarify or modify your communication preferences, please visit us at www.ReaderService.com/consumerschoice or write to us at Harlequin Reader Service Preference Service, P.O. Box 9062, Buffalo, NY 14269. Include your complete name and address.

The Texas Lawman's Woman

by Cathy Gillen Thacker

Welcome to Laramie County, Texas,
where you're bound to run into the first
man you ever loved....

Shelley Meyerson's heart leaped as she caught sight of the broad-shouldered lawman walking out of the dressing room. She blinked, so shocked she nearly fell off the pedestal. "*He's* the best man?"

Colt McCabe locked eyes with Shelley, looking about as pleased as Shelley felt. His chiseled jaw clenched. "Don't tell me *she's* the maid of honor!"

"Now, now, you two," their mutual friend, wedding planner Patricia Wilson, scolded, checking out the fit of Shelley's yellow silk bridesmaid dress. "Surely you can get along for a few days. After all, you're going to have to…since you're both living in Laramie County again."

Don't remind me, Shelley thought with a dramatic sigh.

Looking as handsome as ever in a black tuxedo and pleated white shirt, Colt sized Shelley up. "She's never going to forgive me."

For good reason, Shelley mused, remembering the hurt and humiliation she had suffered as if it were yesterday. She whirled

HAREXP0513

toward Colt so quickly the seamstress stabbed her with a pin. But the pain in her ribs was nothing compared to the pain in her heart. She lifted up her skirt, revealing her favorite pair of cranberry-red cowgirl boots, and stomped off the pedestal, not stopping until they were toe to toe. "You stood me up on prom night, you big galoot!"

Lips thinning, the big, strapping lawman rocked forward on the toes of his boots. "I got there."

Yes, he certainly had, Shelley thought. And even that had been the stuff of Laramie, Texas, legend. The town had talked about it for weeks and weeks. "Two hours late. Unshowered. Unshaven." Shelley threw up her hands in exasperation. "No flowers. No tuxedo…."

Because if he had looked then the way he looked now… Well, who knew what would have happened?

Read more of _THE TEXAS LAWMAN'S WOMAN_ this May 2013, and watch for the rest of this new miniseries McCABE HOMECOMING by Cathy Gillen Thacker. Only from Harlequin® American Romance®!

This cowboy has got trouble written all over him… How can she resist?

Forget cowboys! Ever since she was a girl, India Pike has had an image of the perfect man: sophisticated, refined and with a preference for tailored suits. But after rodeo promoter Liam Parrish came to town, she can't stop mooning over the gorgeous cowboy and single dad. Too bad Liam's totally wrong for her…even if the town's matchmaker already has India saying "I do."

Her Perfect Cowboy
by Trish Milburn

**Available April 23 from
Harlequin® American Romance®.**

Available wherever books are sold.